Scholastic Children's Books
An imprint of Scholastic Ltd
Euston House, 24 Eversholt Street, London, NW1 1DB, UK
Registered office: Westfield Road, Southam, Warwickshire, CV47 0RA
SCHOLASTIC and associated logos are trademarks and/or
registered trademarks of Scholastic Inc.

The Adventures of Captain Underpants
First published in the US by Scholastic Inc, 1997
Copyright © Dav Pilkey, 1997

The Attack of the Talking Toilets
First published in the US by Scholastic Inc, 1999
Copyright © Dav Pilkey, 1999

*The Invasion of the Incredibly Naughty Cafeteria Ladies From Outer Space (and the
Subsequent Assault of the Equally Evil Lunchroom Zombie Nerds)*
First published in the US by Scholastic Inc, 1999
Copyright © Dav Pilkey, 1999

This edition published by Scholastic, 2018

The right of Dav Pilkey to be identified as the author and illustrator of this work
has been asserted by him.

ISBN 978 1407 19253 6

A CIP catalogue record for this book
is available from the British Library.

Printed by CPI Group (UK) Ltd, Croydon, CR0 4YY
Papers used by Scholastic Children's Books are made
from wood grown in sustainable forests.

1 3 5 7 9 10 8 6 4 2

This is a work of fiction. Names, characters, places, incidents
and dialogues are products of the author's imagination or are used
fictitiously. Any resemblance to actual people, living or dead,
events or locales is entirely coincidental.

www.scholastic.co.uk

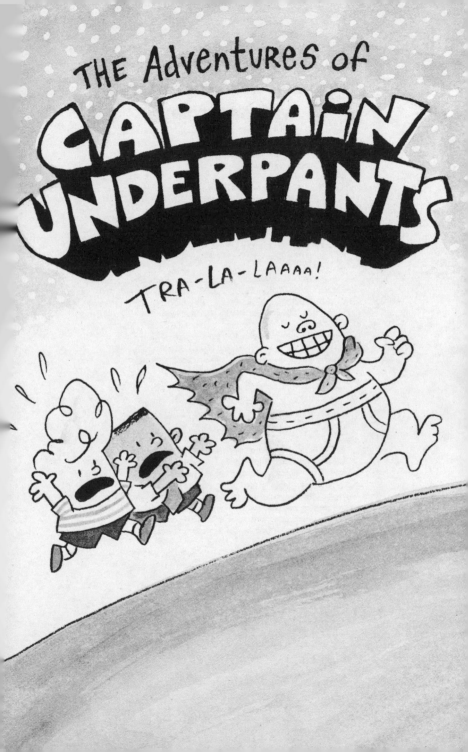

FOR DAVID AND NANCY MELTON
WITH GRATITUDE

CHAPTERS

CHAPTER 1

GEORGE AND HAROLD

Meet George Beard and Harold Hutchins.
George is the kid on the left with the tie and
the flat-top. Harold is the one on the right
with the T-shirt and the bad haircut.
Remember that now.

George and Harold were best friends. They had a lot in common. They lived right next door to each other and they were both in the same fourth-grade class at Jerome Horwitz Elementary School.

George and Harold were usually responsible kids. Whenever anything bad happened, George and Harold were usually responsible.

FLOWER SHOP

PICK OUR

NOSES!

But don't get the wrong idea about these two. George and Harold were actually very nice boys. No matter what everybody else thought, they were good, sweet, and lovable... Well, OK, maybe they weren't so sweet and lovable, but they were good nonetheless.

It's just that George and Harold each had a "silly streak" a *kilometre* long. Usually that silly streak was hard to control. Sometimes it got them into trouble. And once it got them into big, *BIG* trouble.

But before I can tell you that story, I have to tell you *this* story.

CHAPTER 2

TREE HOUSE COMIX, INC.

After a hard day of cracking jokes, pulling pranks, and causing mayhem at school, George and Harold liked to rush to the old tree house in George's backyard. Inside the tree house were two big old fluffy chairs, a table, a cupboard crammed with junk food, and a padlocked crate filled with pencils, pens and stacks and stacks of paper.

Now, Harold loved to draw, and George loved to make up stories. And together, the two boys spent hours and hours writing and drawing their very own comic books.

Over the years, they had created hundreds of their own comics, starring dozens of their own superheroes. First there was "Dog Man", then came "Timmy the Talking Toilet", and who could forget "The Amazing Cow Lady"?

But the all-time greatest superhero they ever made up *had* to be "The Amazing Captain Underpants".

George came up with the idea.

"Most superheroes *look* like they're flying around in their underwear," he said. "Well, this guy actually *is* flying around in his underwear!"

The two boys laughed and laughed.

"Yeah," said Harold, "he could fight with *Wedgie Power*!"

George and Harold spent entire afternoons writing and drawing the comic adventures of Captain Underpants. He was their coolest superhero ever!

Luckily for the boys, the secretary at Jerome Horwitz Elementary School was much too busy to keep an eye on the photo-copier. So whenever they got a chance, Harold and George would sneak into the office and run off several hundred copies of their latest Captain Underpants adventure.

After school, they sold their homemade comics on the playground for 50¢ each.

captain Underpants was faster than a speeding WAISTBAND...
ZOOM
MORE Powerful than Boxer Shorts...
And ABLE to LEAP tall Bildings without getting a wedgie.
TRA-LA LAAAA!
Night and Day, CAPTAIN UNDERPANTS watched over the city, fighting for truth, JUSTISE, And ALL that is PRE-SHRUNK and cottony.
Meanwhile, At a nearby elementery school...
Turn the Page

CHAPTER 4

MEAN OLD MR KRUPP

Do you see that old guy
looking out of the window
up there?
That's Mr Krupp,
the principal.

Now, Mr Krupp was the meanest, sourest old principal in the whole history of Jerome Horwitz Elementary School. He hated laughter and singing. He hated the sounds of children playing at break-time. In fact, he hated children altogether!

And guess which two children Mr Krupp hated most of all?

If you guessed George and Harold, you're right! Mr Krupp *hated* George and Harold.

He hated their pranks and their wise-cracks. He hated their silly attitudes and their constant giggling. And he especially hated those awful *Captain Underpants* comic books.

"I'm going to get those boys one day,"
Mr Krupp vowed. "One day very, very soon!"

CHAPTER 5

ONE DAY VERY, VERY SOON

Remember when I said that George and Harold's "silly streak" got them into big, *BIG* trouble once? Well, this is the story of how that happened. And how some huge pranks (and a little blackmail) turned their principal into the coolest superhero of all time.

It was the day of the big football game between the Horwitz Knuckleheads and the Stubinville Stinkbugs. The stands were packed with fans.

The cheerleaders ran on to the field and shook their pom-poms over their heads.

A fine black dust drifted out of their pom-poms and settled all around them.

"Gimme a K!" shouted the cheerleaders.

"*K!*" repeated the fans.

"Gimme an N!" shouted the cheerleaders.

"*N!*" repeated the fans.

"Gimme an . . . a-ah-ah-A-CHOO!" sneezed the cheerleaders.

"*A-ah-ah-A-CHOO!*" repeated the fans.

A-CHOO
ACHOO
ACHOOO

The cheerleaders sneezed and sneezed
and sneezed some more. They couldn't stop
sneezing.

"Hey!" shouted a fan in the stands.
"Somebody sprinkled black pepper into the
cheerleaders' pom-poms!"

"I wonder who did that?" asked another fan.

The cheerleaders stumbled off the field, sneezing and dripping with mucus, as the marching band members took their places.

But when the band began to play, steady streams of bubbles began blowing out of their instruments! Bubbles were *everywhere*! Up and down the field the marching band slipped and slid, leaving behind a thick trail of wet, bubbly foam.

"Hey!" shouted a fan in the stands. "Somebody poured bubble bath into the marching band's instruments!"

"I wonder who did that?" asked another fan.

Soon, the football teams took the field. The Knuckleheads kicked the ball. Up, up, up went the ball. Higher and higher it went. The ball sailed into the clouds and kept right on going until nobody could see it any more.

"Hey!" shouted a fan in the stands. "Somebody filled the game ball with *helium*!"

"I wonder who did that?" asked another fan.

But the missing ball didn't make any difference because at that moment, the Knuckleheads were rolling around the field, scratching and itching like crazy.

"Hey!" shouted the coach. "Somebody replaced our Deep-Heating Muscle Rub Lotion with Mr Prankster's Extra-Scratchy Itching Cream!"

"We wonder who did that?!" shouted the fans in the stands.

The whole afternoon went on much the same way, with people shouting everything from "Hey, somebody put Sea-Monkeys in the lemonade!" to "Hey, somebody glued all the bathroom doors shut!"

Before long, most of the fans in the stands had left. The big game had been forfeited, and everyone in the entire school was *miserable*.

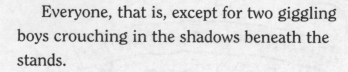

Everyone, that is, except for two giggling boys crouching in the shadows beneath the stands.

"Those were our best pranks yet!" laughed Harold.

"Yep," chuckled George, "they'll be hard to top, that's for sure."

"I just hope we don't get busted for this," said Harold.

"Don't worry," said George. "We covered our tracks really well. There's *no way* we'll get busted!"

CHAPTER 6

BUSTED

The next day at school, an announcement came over the loudspeakers.

"George Beard and Harold Hutchins, please report to Principal Krupp's office at once."

"Uh-oh!" said Harold. "I don't like the sound of *that*!"

"Don't worry," said George. "They can't prove anything!"

George and Harold entered Principal Krupp's office and sat down on the chairs in front of his desk. The two boys had been in this office together countless times before, but this time was different. Mr Krupp was *smiling*. As long as George and Harold had known Mr Krupp, they had never, *ever* seen him smile. Mr Krupp knew something.

"I didn't see you boys at the big game yesterday," said Mr Krupp.

"Uh, no," said George. "We weren't feeling well."

"Y-Y-Yeah," Harold stammered nervously. "W-W-We went home."

"Aw, that's too bad," said Principal Krupp. "You boys missed a good game."

George and Harold quickly glanced at each other, gulped, and tried hard not to look guilty.

"Lucky for you, I have a videotape of the whole thing," Mr Krupp said. He turned on the television in the corner and pressed the play button on the VCR.

A black-and-white image appeared on the
TV screen. It was an overhead shot of George
and Harold sprinkling pepper into the cheerleaders' pom-poms. Next came a shot of
George and Harold pouring liquid bubble
bath into the marching band's instruments.

"How do you like the *pre-game show*?"
asked Mr Krupp with a devilish grin.

George eyed the television screen in terror. He couldn't answer. Harold's eyes were glued to the floor. He couldn't look.

The tape went on and on, revealing all of George and Harold's "behind the scenes" antics. By now, both boys were eyeing the floor, squirming nervously, and dripping with sweat.

Mr Krupp turned off the TV.

"You know," he said, "ever since you boys came to this school, it's been one prank after another. First you put dissected frogs in the salad at the parent-teacher banquet. Then you made it snow in the cafeteria. Then you rigged all the intercoms so they played "Weird Al" Yankovic songs *full blast* for six hours straight.

"For *four long years* you two have been running amok in this school, and I've never been able to prove anything – until now!"

Mr Krupp held the videotape in his hand. "I took the liberty of installing tiny video surveillance cameras all around the school. I knew I'd catch you two in the act one day. I just didn't know it would be *so easy*!"

CHAPTER 7

A LITTLE BLACKMAIL

Mr Krupp sat back in his chair and chuckled to himself for a long, long time. Finally, George got up the courage to speak.

"W-What are you going to do with that tape?" he said.

"I thought you'd never ask," laughed Principal Krupp.

"I've thought long and hard about what to do with this tape," Mr Krupp said. "At first, I thought I'd send copies to your parents."

The boys swallowed hard and sank deeply into their chairs.

"Then I thought I might send a copy to the school board," Mr Krupp continued. "I could get you both *expelled* for this!"

The boys swallowed harder and sank deeper into their chairs.

"Finally, I came to a decision," Mr Krupp concluded. "I think the football team would be very curious to find out just *who* was responsible for yesterday's fiasco. I think I'll send a copy to them!"

George and Harold leaped out of their chairs and fell to their knees.

"No!" cried George. "You can't do that. They'll *kill* us!"

"Yeah," begged Harold, "they'll kill us every day for the rest of our lives!"

Mr Krupp laughed and laughed.

"Please have mercy," the boys cried. "We'll do anything!"

"Anything?" asked Principal Krupp with delight. He reached into his desk, pulled out a list of demands, and tossed it at the boys. "If you don't want to be *dead as long as you live*, you'll follow these rules *exactly*!"

George and Harold carefully looked over the list.

"This . . . this is blackmail!" said George.

"Call it what you like," Principal Krupp snapped, "but if you two don't follow that list *exactly*, then this tape becomes the property of the Horwitz Knuckleheads!"

#22
#13 A
#7. NO

RULES

#1. NO MORE PRACTICAL JOKES OR PRANKS

#2. NO LAUGHING OR SMILING

#3. NO MORE T

#4. NO MORE CAPTAIN UNDERP

#5. WASH MY CAR EVE

#6. MOW MY

CHAPTER 8

CRIME AND PUNISHMENT

At six o'clock the next morning, George and Harold dragged themselves out of bed, walked over to Mr Krupp's house, and began washing his car.

Then, while Harold scrubbed the tyres, George roamed around the yard pulling up all the weeds and nettles he could find. After-wards, they cleaned the gutters and washed all the windows on Mr Krupp's house.

At school, George and Harold sat up
straight, listened carefully, and spoke only
when spoken to. They didn't tell jokes, they
didn't pull pranks – they didn't even smile.

Their teacher kept pinching herself. "I just
know this is a dream," she said.

At lunch, the two boys vacuumed Mr. Krupp's office, shined his shoes, and polished his desktop. At break, they clipped his finger-nails and ironed his tie.

Each spare moment in the boys' daily schedule was spent catering to Mr Krupp's every whim.

After school, George and Harold mowed Mr Krupp's lawn, tended his garden, and began painting the front of his house. At sunset, Mr Krupp came outside and handed each boy a stack of books.

"Gentlemen," he said, "I've asked your teachers to give you *both* extra homework. Now go home, study hard, and I'll see you back here at six o'clock tomorrow morning. We've got a busy day ahead of us."

"Thank you, sir," moaned the two boys.

George and Harold walked home dead tired.

"Man, this was the worst day of my entire life," said George.

"Don't worry," said Harold. "We only have to do this for eight more years. Then we can move away to some far-off land where they'll never find us. Maybe Antarctica."

"I've got a better idea," said George.

He took a piece of paper out of his pocket
and handed it to Harold. It was an old maga-
zine ad for a 3-D Hypno-Ring.

"How's *this* going to help us?" asked
Harold.

"All we gotta do is hypnotize Mr Krupp,"
said George. "We'll make him give us the
video and forget this whole mess ever happened."

"That's a great idea!" said Harold. "And the
best part is we only have to wait four-to-six
weeks for delivery!"

CHAPTER 9

FOUR-TO-SIX
WEEKS LATER

After four-to-six weeks of backbreaking slave labour, gruelling homework assignments, and humiliating good behaviour at school, a package arrived in George's mailbox from the Li'l Wiseguy Novelty Company.

It was the 3-D Hypno-Ring.

51

"Hallelujah!" cried George. "It's everything I ever hoped for!"

"Let me see, let me see," said Harold.

"Don't look directly at it," warned George. "You don't want to get hypnotized, do you?"

"Do you really think it will work?" asked Harold. "Do you really think we can 'amaze our friends, control our enemies, and take over the world' just like the ad says?"

"It better work," said George. "Or else we've just wasted four whole bucks!"

CHAPTER 10

THE 3-D HYPNO-RING

The next morning, George and Harold didn't arrive early at Mr Krupp's house to wash his car and reshingle his roof. In fact, they were even a little late getting to school.

When they finally turned up, Mr Krupp was standing at the front door waiting for them. And boy, was he *angry!*

Mr Krupp escorted the boys into his office and slammed the door.

"All right, where were you two this morning?" he growled.

"We wanted to come over to your house," said George, "but we were busy trying to figure out the secret of this *ring*."

"What ring?" snapped Mr Krupp.

George held up his hand and showed the ring to Principal Krupp.

"It's got one of those weird patterns on it," said Harold. "If you stare at it long enough, a picture appears."

"Well, hold it still," snarled Mr Krupp. "I can't see the darn thing!"

"I have to move it back and forth," said George, "or else it won't work."

Mr Krupp's eyes followed the ring back
and forth, back and forth, back and forth, and
back and forth.

"You have to stare deeper into the ring,"
said Harold. "Deeper . . . deeeper . . . deeeeper
. . . deeeeeeeeeper."

"You are getting sleepy," said George.
"Veeeeery sleeeeeeeeeepy."

Mr Krupp's eyelids began to droop.
"I'mmmsssooooosssleeepy," he mumbled.

After a few minutes, Mr Krupp's eyes were
closed tight, and he began to snore.

"You are under our spell," said George.
"When I snap my fingers, you will obey our
every command!"

Snap!

"Iwwillllloobeyyy," mumbled Mr Krupp.

"All right," said George. "Have you still got that videotape of me and Harold?"

"Yeeessss," mumbled Mr Krupp.

"Well, hand it over, bub," George instructed.

Mr Krupp unlocked a large filing cabinet and opened the bottom drawer. He reached in and handed George the videotape. George stuffed it into his backpack.

Harold took a *different* video out of his backpack and put it into the filing cabinet.

"What's that video?" asked George.

"It's one of my little sister's old 'Boomer the Purple Dragon Sing-A-Long' videos."

"Nice touch," said George.

CHAPTER 11

FUN WITH HYPNOSIS

When Harold bent down to close the filing
cabinet, he took a quick look inside.

"Whoa!" he cried. "Look at all the stuff in
here!"

The filing cabinet was filled with everything Mr Krupp had taken away from the boys
over the years. There were slingshots,
whoopee cushions, skateboards, fake doggy
doo-doo – you name it, it was in there.

"Look at this!" cried George. "A big stack
of *Captain Underpants* comics!"

"He's got every issue!" said Harold.

For hours, the two boys sat on the floor laughing and reading their comics. Finally, George looked up at the clock.

"Yikes!" he said. "It's almost lunchtime! We better clean up this mess and get to class."

The boys looked up at their principal, who had been standing behind them in a trance all morning.

"Gee, I almost forgot about Mr Krupp," said Harold. "What should we do with him?"

"Do you want to have some fun?" asked George.

"Why not?" said Harold. "I haven't had *any* fun in the last four-to-six weeks!"

"Cool," said George. He walked up to Mr Krupp and snapped his fingers. *Snap!* "You are—a *chicken*!" he said.

Suddenly, Mr Krupp leaped on to his desk and flapped his arms. "Cluck, cluck, cluck-cluck," he cried, kicking his papers off the desk behind him and pecking at his pen-and-pencil set.

George and Harold howled with laughter.

"Let me try, let me try," said Harold.

"Ummm, you are a – a *monkey*!"

"You gotta snap your fingers," said George.

"Oh, yeah," said Harold. *Snap!* "You are a
monkey!"

Suddenly, Mr Krupp sprang off his desk
and began swinging from the fluorescent
light fixtures. "Ooo-ooo, ooo-oooo, OOOOO!"
he shrieked, leaping from one side of the
room to the other.

George and Harold laughed so hard they
almost cried.

"My turn, my turn!" said George. "Let's see. What should we turn him into next?"

"I know," Harold said, holding up a *Captain Underpants* comic. "Let's turn him into Captain Underpants!"

"Good idea," said George. *Snap!* "You are now the greatest superhero of all time: *The Amazing Captain Underpants*!"

Mr Krupp tore down the red curtain from his office window and tied it around his neck. Then he took off his shoes, socks, shirt, trousers and his awful toupee.

"Tra-La-Laaaaaaaa!" he sang.

Mr Krupp stood before them looking quite triumphant, with his cape blowing in the breeze of the open window. George and Harold were dumbfounded.

"You know," said George, "he kinda *looks* like Captain Underpants."

"Yeah," Harold replied.

After a short silence, the two boys looked at each other and burst into laughter. George and Harold had never laughed so hard in all their lives. Tears ran down their faces as they rolled about the floor, shrieking in hysterics.

After a while, George pulled himself up from the floor for another look.

"Hey," George cried. "Where'd he go?"

CHAPTER 12

OUT OF THE WINDOW

George and Harold dashed to the window and looked out. There, running across the car park, was a pudgy old guy in his underwear with a red cape flowing behind him.

TRA-LA-LAAA!

"Mr Krupp, come back!" shouted Harold.

"He won't answer to *that*," said George. "He thinks he's Captain Underpants now."

"Oh, no," said Harold.

"He's probably running off to fight crime," said George.

"Oh, *no*," said Harold.

"And we gotta stop him," said George.

"Oh, NO," cried Harold. *"NO WAY!"*

"Look," said George, "he could get *killed* out there."

Harold was unmoved.

"Or worse," said George. "We could get into BIG trouble!"

"You're right," said Harold. "We *gotta* go after him!"

The two boys opened the bottom cabinet drawer and took out their slingshots and skateboards.

"Do you think we should bring anything else?" asked Harold.

"Yeah," said George. "Let's bring the fake doggy doo-doo."

"Good thinking," said Harold. "You just never know when fake doggy doo-doo is going to come in handy!"

Harold stuffed Mr Krupp's clothes, shoes
and toupee into his backpack. Then together
the two boys leaped out of the window, slid
down the flagpole, and took off on their skateboards after the Amazing Captain Underpants.

CHAPTER 13

BANK ROBBERS

George and Harold rode their skateboards all over town looking for Captain Underpants.

"I can't find him anywhere," said Harold.

"You'd think a guy like him would be *easy* to spot," said George.

Then the boys turned a corner, and *there*
he was. Captain Underpants – standing in
front of a bank, looking quite heroic.

"Mr Krupp!" cried Harold.

"Shhh," said George, "don't call him that.
Call him Captain Underpants!"

"Oh, yeah," said Harold.

"And don't forget to snap your fingers,"
said George.

"Right!" said Harold.

But before he got a chance, the bank doors flew wide open, and out stepped two robbers. The robbers took one look at Captain Underpants and stopped dead in their tracks.

"Surrender!" said Captain Underpants. "Or I will have to resort to *Wedgie Power*!"

"Oh, no," whispered Harold and George.

Nobody moved for about ten seconds. Finally, the robbers looked at each other and burst out laughing. They dropped their loot and fell to the pavement screaming in hysterics.

Almost immediately, the cops arrived and arrested the crooks.

"Let that be a lesson to you," cried Captain Underpants. "Never underestimate the power of underwear!"

The police chief, looking quite angry, marched over to Captain Underpants.

"And just who the heck are *you* supposed to be?" the police chief demanded.

"Why, *I'm* Captain Underpants, the world's greatest superhero," said Captain Underpants. "I fight for Truth, Justice and *all* that is Pre-Shrunk and Cottony!"

"Oh, *YEAH*!!?" shouted the police chief. "Cuff him, boys!"

One of the cops took out his handcuffs and grabbed Captain Underpants by the arm.

"Uh-oh!" cried George. "We gotta roll!"
Together the two boys zoomed into the
crowd, weaving in and out of cops and
bystanders. Harold skated up to Captain
Underpants and knocked the superhero off his
feet. George caught him and the boys skated
away with Captain Underpants on their shoulders.

"Stop!" cried the cops, but it was too late.
George, Harold and Captain Underpants were
gone.

CHAPTER 14

THE BIG BANG

After their quick escape, George, Harold, and Captain Underpants stopped on a deserted street corner to catch their breath.

"OK," said George. "Let's de-hypnotize him quick, before something else . . .

. . . happens!"

KA-BOOM

A huge explosion came from the Rare
Crystal Shop across the street. Heavy smoke
poured out of the building. Suddenly, two
robots with one stolen crystal emerged from
the smoke and jumped into an old van.

"Did I just see two *ROBOTS* get into a
van?" asked Harold.

"You know," said George, "up until *now*
this story was almost *believable*!"

"Well, believable or not," said Harold, "we're not getting involved. I repeat: We are *NOT* getting involved!"

Just then, Captain Underpants leaped from the street corner and dashed in front of the van.

"Stop, in the name of underwear!" he cried.

"Uh-oh," said George. "I think we're *involved*."

The two robots started up the van and swerved around Captain Underpants. Unfortunately, the van brushed up against his red cape, and it got caught. With a mighty *jerk*, Captain Underpants flipped backward, and the van pulled him along as it drove away.

"GRAB HIM!" cried George.

The two boys skateboarded with all their might towards the speeding van and grabbed Captain Underpants by the ankles.

"HEEEEEEELLLLLLLP!" they cried as the van pulled them through the city streets.

"Mummy," said a little boy sitting on a bench, "I just saw two robots driving a van with a guy in his underwear hanging off the back by a red cape, pulling two boys on skateboards behind him with his feet."

"How do you expect me to believe such a ridiculous story?" asked his mother.

Finally, the van came to a screeching halt in front of an old abandoned warehouse. The sudden stop made Captain Underpants flip over the roof of the van and crash through the front door of the building.

"Well, well, well," said a strange voice from inside the warehouse. "It looks as if we have a *visitor*."

CHAPTER 15

DR NAPPY

George and Harold hid behind the van until
the coast was clear. Then they sneaked up to
the hole in the door and peeked inside.

Captain Underpants was all tied up, the
two robots were standing guard, and a strange
little man wearing a nappy was laughing
maniacally.

"I am the evil Dr Nappy," the strange little man told Captain Underpants. "And you will be the first to witness my takeover of the *world*!"

Dr Nappy placed the stolen crystal into a large machine called the *Laser-Matic 2000*. The machine started to light up and make loud noises. Heavy gears began shifting and spinning, and a laser beam from the crystal shot straight up through a hole in the roof.

"In exactly twenty minutes, this laser beam will blow up the moon and send huge chunks of it crashing down upon every major city in the world!" laughed Dr Nappy. "Then, I will rise from the rubble and take over the planet!"

"Only one thing can help us now," said George.

"What?" asked Harold.

"Rubber doggy doo-doo," said George.

Harold took the fake doggy doo-doo and a
slingshot from George's backpack and handed
them to him.

"Be careful," said Harold. "The fate of the
entire planet is in your hands!"

With careful and precise aim, George shot
the rubber doo-doo through the air and
across the room. It landed with a *plop*! – right
at the feet of Dr Nappy.

"Yessss!" whispered George and Harold.

Dr Nappy looked down at the doo-doo
between his feet and turned bright red.

"Oh, dear me!" he cried. "I'm dreadfully
embarrassed! Please excuse me."

He began to waddle towards the toilet.
"This has never happened to me before, I
assure you," he said. "I-I guess with all the
excitement, I just . . . I just. . . Oh, dear! Oh,
dear!"

While Dr Nappy was off changing himself, George and Harold sneaked into the old ware-house.

Immediately, the robots detected the boys and began marching toward them. "Destroy the intruders!" said the robots. "Destroy the intruders!"

George and Harold screamed and ran to the back of the warehouse. Luckily, George found two old boards and gave one of them to Harold.

"We're not going to have to resort to extremely graphic violence, are we?" asked Harold.

"I sure hope not," said George.

CHAPTER 16

THE EXTREMELY GRAPHIC VIOLENCE CHAPTER

WARNING:

The following chapter contains graphic scenes showing two boys beating the tar out of a couple of robots.

If you have high blood pressure, or if you faint at the sight of motor oil, we strongly urge you to take better care of yourself and stop being such a baby.

Introducing
FLIP-
As everybody knows, nothing enhances silly action sequences more than cheesy animation.
And so, for the first time in the history of great literature, we proudly bring you the latest in cheesy animation technology: The art of Flip-O-Rama.

PILKEY® BRAND

RAMA

HERE'S HOW IT WORKS!

Step 1
Place your *left* hand inside the dotted lines marked "LEFT HAND HERE." Hold the book open *flat*.

Step 2
Grasp the *right-hand* page with your right thumb and index finger (inside the dotted lines marked "RIGHT THUMB HERE")

Step 3
Now *quickly* flip the right-hand page back and forth until the picture appears to be *animated*.

(For extra fun, try adding your own sound-effects!)

FLIP-O-RAMA 1

(pages 89 and 91)

Remember, flip *only* page 89.
While you are flipping, be sure you
can see the picture on page 89
and the one on page 91.
If you flip quickly, the two
pictures will start to look like
<u>one</u> *animated* picture.

Don't forget to
add your own sound-effects!

LEFT HAND HERE

ROBOT RAMPAGE!

RIGHT
THUMB
HERE

ROBOT RAMPAGE!

FLIP-O-RAMA 2

(pages 93 and 95)

Remember, flip *only* page 93.
While you are flipping, be sure you
can see the picture on page 93
and the one on page 95.
If you flip quickly, the two
pictures will start to look like
<u>one</u> *animated* picture.

Don't forget to
add your own sound-effects!

LEFT HAND HERE

GEORGE SAVES HAROLD!

RIGHT
THUMB
HERE

GEORGE SAVES HAROLD!

FLIP-O-RAMA 3

(pages 97 and 99)

Remember, flip *only* page 97.
While you are flipping, be sure you
can see the picture on page 97
and the one on page 99.
If you flip quickly, the two
pictures will start to look like
<u>one</u> *animated* picture.

Don't forget to
add your own sound-effects!

LEFT HAND HERE

HAROLD RETURNS THE FAVOUR!

RIGHT
THUMB
HERE

HAROLD RETURNS
THE FAVOUR!

FLIP-O-RAMA 4

(pages 101 and 103)

Remember, flip *only* page 101.
While you are flipping, be sure you
can see the picture on page 101
and the one on page 103.
If you flip quickly, the two
pictures will start to look like
<u>one</u> *animated* picture.

Don't forget to
add your own sound-effects!

LEFT HAND HERE

MIXED NUTS
(...AND BOLTS!)

RIGHT
THUMB
HERE

MIXED NUTS
(...AND BOLTS!)

CHAPTER 17

THE ESCAPE

After defeating the robots, George and Harold untied Captain Underpants.

"Come on!" cried Harold. "Let's get out of here!"

"Wait!" said Captain Underpants. "We have to save the world first!"

So George, Harold and Captain Underpants frantically looked all over the *Laser-Matic 2000*, searching for a way to shut it down and stop the inevitable disaster.

ON

"Ummm," said Harold. "I think *this* might be the lever we want."

He pulled the "Self-Destruct" lever with all his might. Suddenly, the *Laser-Matic 2000* began to sputter and shake. The huge laser beam turned off, and pieces of the machine began flying off in all directions.

"It's gonna BLOW!" cried Harold. "RUN FOR YOUR LIVES!"

SELF-
DESTRUCT
(PLEASE
DON'T PULL)

"*NOT SO FAST!*" screamed Dr Nappy, who had appeared out of nowhere. "You demolished my robots. You *destroyed* my *Laser-Matic 2000*. And you ruined my one chance to take over the world – but you won't live to tell the tale!" Dr Nappy pulled out his *Nappy-Matic 2000* ray gun, and pointed it at George, Harold and Captain Underpants.

Captain Underpants quickly stretched a
pair of underwear and shot it at Dr Nappy.
The underwear landed right on the evil doctor's head.

"Help!" cried Dr Nappy. "I can't see! I can't
see!"

George and Harold ran out of the warehouse as fast as they could.

"Great shot, Captain Underpants!" cried
Harold.

"There's just one thing I don't under-
stand," said George. "Where'd you get the
extra pair of underwear?"

"What extra pair?" said Captain
Underpants.

"Never mind that," cried George, "let's just get out of here before that *Laser-Matic 2000* thing ex . . .

. . . plodes!"

The *Laser-Matic 2000* blew up, tearing apart the old warehouse. It sent flaming shards of red-hot metal in every direction. Fire fell from the skies around our heroes, and the earth began to crumble beneath their feet.

"Oh, NO!" cried Harold. *"WE'RE DOOMED!"*

CHAPTER 18

TO MAKE A LONG STORY SHORT

They got away.

CHAPTER 19

BACK TO SCHOOL

George, Harold and Captain Underpants made a quick stop outside the police station. They tied Dr Nappy to a lamppost and attached a note to him.

"There!" said Captain Underpants. "That ought to explain everything."

Then George and Harold led Captain Underpants back to Jerome Horwitz Elementary School.

"Why are we going *here*?" asked Captain Underpants.

"Well," said George, "you have to do some *undercover* work."

"Yeah," said Harold, reaching into his backpack. "Put these clothes on, and make it snappy!"

"Don't forget your hair," said George.

Captain Underpants quickly got dressed behind some bushes. "Well, how do I look?" he asked.

"Pretty good," said George. "Now try to look really angry!"

Captain Underpants made the nastiest face he could.

"You know," said Harold, "he kinda looks like Mr Krupp!"

"*Harold,*" whispered George, "he is Mr Krupp!"

"Oh, yeah," said Harold. "I almost forgot."

Before long, they were all back inside Mr
Krupp's office.

"OK, Captain Underpants," said George,
"you are now Mr Krupp."

"Snap your fingers," whispered Harold.

"Oh, yeah," said George. *Snap!* "You are
now Mr Krupp."

"Who's Mr Krupp?" asked Captain
Underpants.

"*Oh, NO!*" cried Harold. "*It's not working!*"

The boys tried again and again to de-hypnotize Captain Underpants, but *nothing*
seemed to work.

"Hmmm," said Harold. "Let me see the instruction manual for that ring."

George checked his trouser pocket.

"Umm," said George, "I think I *lost* it."

"You WHAT?" cried Harold. The two boys searched frantically through the office, but the 3-D Hypno-Ring instruction manual was nowhere to be found.

"Never mind," said George. "I have an idea." He removed the flowers from a large vase in the corner. Then he poured out all of the water over Captain Underpants' head.

"What did you do *that* for?" cried Harold.

"I saw 'em do this in a cartoon once," said George, "so it's *gotta* work!"

After a few minutes, Mr Krupp slowly came to. "What's going on here?" he demanded. "And why am I all wet!!?"

George and Harold had never been so glad to see Mr Krupp in all their lives.

"I'm so happy I could cry," said Harold.

"Well, you're *gonna* cry when I give that videotape to the football team!" shouted Mr Krupp. "I've *had it* with you two!"

Principal Krupp took the videotape out of his filing cabinet. "You boys are *dead meat*!" he sneered. He stormed out of his office with the video and headed towards the gym.

George and Harold smiled. "Wait till the football team sees *that* video!" said Harold.

"Yeah," said George, "I sure hope they like singing purple dragons!"

"Hey, look," said George. "I found the 3-D Hypno-Ring instruction manual. It was in my *shirt* pocket, not my trouser pocket!"

"Well, throw that thing away," said Harold. "We'll never need it again."

"I certainly hope not," said George.

WARNING!!!
Whatever you do, don't put water on anybody's head when they are in a trance! This will cause the hypnotized person to slip back and forth from trance to reality whenever they hear the sound of fingers snapping.

TRASH

CHAPTER 20

THE END?

Things at Jerome Horwitz Elementary School
were never quite the same after that fateful day.

The football team enjoyed Mr Krupp's
video so much that they changed their name
from the Knuckleheads to the Purple Dragon
Sing-A-Long Friends. The name change didn't
go down too well with the fans, but hey, who's
going to argue with a bunch of linebackers?

George and Harold went back to their old
ways, pulling pranks, cracking jokes and
making new comic books.

They had to keep an eye on Mr Krupp,
though . . .

. . . because for some *strange* reason, every time he heard the sound of fingers snapping . . .

Snap!

. . . Principal Krupp turned *back* into . . .

. . . you know who!

"Oh, no!" cried Harold.
"Here we go *again*!" said George.

FOR DAVID AND NANCY MELTON
WITH GRATITUDE

FOR ALAN BOYKO

CHAPTERS

Um...hello.
Before you read this book, there are some things you should know...
So Harold and I have created this informative pamphlet to fill you in on the details.
Please don't let this comic fall into the wrong hands.

CHAPTER 1

GEORGE AND HAROLD

This is George Beard and Harold Hutchins.
George is the kid on the left with the tie
and the flat-top. Harold is the one on the
right with the T-shirt and the bad haircut.
Remember that now.

Depending on who you asked, you'd probably hear a lot of different things about George and Harold.

Their teacher, Ms Ribble, might say that George and Harold were *disruptive* and *behaviourally challenged*.

Their gym teacher, Mr Meaner, might add that they were in serious need of a major *attitude adjustment*.

Their principal, Mr Krupp, would probably have a few more choice words to include, like *sneaky*, and *criminally mischievous*, and *"I'll get those boys if it's the last thing I . . ."* Well, you get the idea.

But if you asked their parents, they'd probably tell you that George and Harold were smart and sweet, and very good-hearted . . . even if they were a bit silly at times.

I'd have to agree with their parents.

But even so, their silliness *did* get them into a lot of trouble sometimes. In fact, it once got them into so much trouble, they accidentally almost destroyed the whole planet with an army of evil, vicious talking toilets!

But before I can tell you that story, I have to tell you *this* story. . .

CHAPTER 2

THIS STORY

One fine morning at Jerome Horwitz
Elementary School, George and Harold
had just left their fourth-grade remedial
PE class when they saw a big sign in the
hallway.

It was an announcement for the Second
Annual *Invention Convention*.

George and Harold had fond memories of last year's Invention Convention, but this year's convention was a bit different. The first-prize winner got to be "Principal for the Day".

"Wow," said George. "Whoever gets to be principal gets to make up all the rules for the whole day, and everybody in school has to follow those rules!"

"We have *got* to win first prize this year!" exclaimed Harold.

Just then, George and Harold's principal,
Mr Krupp, showed up.

"A-HA!" he shouted. "I'll bet you two are
up to no good!"

"Not really," said George. "We were just
reading about this year's contest."

"Yeah," said Harold. "We're going to win
first prize in the contest and be *Principals
for the Day*!"

"Ha, ha, ha, ha, ha!" laughed Mr Krupp. "Do you *honestly* think I'd let you two enter this year's contest after that stunt you pulled at *last* year's Invention Convention?!!?"

George and Harold smiled and thought back to the First Annual Invention Convention. . .

CHAPTER 3

THE FLASHBACK

It was about one year earlier, and all of the faculty and students of Jerome Horwitz Elementary School had gathered in the gymnasium for what would later be known as the "Sticky Chair Incident". George and Harold stepped up to the microphone.

"Ladies and gentlemen," said George,
"Harold and I have invented something
that is guaranteed to keep you all *glued to
your seats*!"

"Yes," said Harold. "We call it *glue*."

Mr Krupp became very angry. "You two
did not invent *glue*!" he shouted. He stood
up to take the microphone away from
Harold, and his chair stood up with him.
Everyone in the gymnasium laughed.

The school secretary, Miss Anthrope,
stood up to help remove Mr Krupp's chair
from his trousers. Her chair stood up with
her, too. Everyone in the gymnasium
laughed harder.

The other teachers stood up, and — you guessed it — they were stuck to their chairs as well. Everyone in the audience howled with laughter.

One kid stood up to go to the toilet, and his chair came up with him, also. The audience stopped laughing so hard. They all quickly checked their chairs.

Suddenly the laughter stopped completely. Everyone in the whole school was glued to their seats.

You see, while it was true that George
and Harold had not invented glue, they *had*
invented a new *kind* of glue. By simply
mixing putty with concentrated orange
juice mix, they had created a quick-drying,
body-heat-activated glue. Then they had
applied this special glue to every seat in the
gymnasium (except theirs) early that
morning.

Everybody in the gymnasium was
glaring at George and Harold and *seething*
with anger.

"I've got a good idea," said George.

"What?" asked Harold.

"RUN!!!" cried George.

George and Harold were grinning from ear to ear, remembering their silly invention and the chaos that followed.

"That was hilarious," laughed Harold.

"Yeah," chuckled George. "It'll be hard to top that *this* year!"

"Well, you won't get a chance this year," said Mr Krupp. He took out a magnifying glass and held it up to the fine print on the sign.

"This contest is open to all students in the third and fourth grades EXCEPT George Beard and Harold Hutchins. . . "

"You mean, we can't enter the contest?" asked Harold.

"It's worse than that," laughed Mr Krupp. "You boys can't even *attend* this year's convention. I'm putting you two in study hall that whole day!" Mr Krupp turned and walked away, laughing victoriously.

"Rats!" said Harold. "What are we going to do now?"

"Well," said George, "you know the old saying: If you can't join 'em, *beat 'em*!"

CHAPTER 4

THE INVENTION

Early that evening, George and Harold
sneaked back to school with their supplies.
They crept into the gymnasium and peeked
around.

"I think somebody's still in here,"
whispered Harold.

"Oh, it's just Melvin Sneedly," said
George.

Melvin was the school brainiac. He was
busy putting some last-minute touches on
his new invention for the contest.

"We should wait here until he leaves," whispered Harold.

"No way," said George. "He could be here all night! Let's just go over and talk to him."

When Melvin saw George and Harold approaching, he was not happy. "Oh, *no*!" he said. "I'll bet you guys are here to mess with everybody's inventions."

"Nice guess," said George. "Listen, we promise not to mess with *your* invention, if you promise not to tell anybody that you saw *us* here tonight."

Melvin looked lovingly at his invention, and reluctantly agreed. "I promise," he said.

ELECTR
APPLE

JTO-
TIC
OE

28

"Great," said George. "What is that invention of yours, anyway? It just looks like a photocopy machine."

"Well, it *used* to be a photocopy machine," said Melvin, "but I've made some major adjustments to it. Now it is an invention that will revolutionize the world. I call it the PATSY 2000."

"It'll revolutionize the world, and you named it *PATSY*???" asked Harold.

"Yes," said Melvin. "PATSY is an acronym for Photo-Atomic Trans-Somgobulating Yectofantriplutoniczanziptomiser."

"I'm sorry I asked," said Harold.

"Allow me to demonstrate," said Melvin. "The PATSY 2000 can take any one-dimensional image and create a living, breathing, three-dimensional copy of that image. For example, take this ordinary photograph of a mouse."

Melvin placed the photo of the mouse on to the glass screen of the PATSY 2000 and pressed Start.

The lights in the gymnasium dimmed as all the power in the entire school seemed to get sucked into the PATSY 2000. Soon the machine began to vibrate and hum loudly, and tiny bolts of static electricity snapped out from underneath.

"I hope that thing doesn't explode," said
Harold.

"Oh, this is *nothing*," said Melvin. "You
should have seen how the PATSY 2000
reacted when I copied a *poodle*!"

Finally, after a series of flashes and loud
zaps, everything stopped. A small *ding* was
heard, then a tiny mouse crawled out of the
side door of the PATSY 2000 and on to the
floor.

"Isn't it wonderful?" exclaimed Melvin.

George inspected the mouse closely.

"That's a great trick," George laughed. "You really had me goin' for a while!"

"It's *not* a trick," cried Melvin. "The PATSY 2000 really *does* bring photos to life! I've even created living creatures from *paintings and drawings*!"

"Yeah, *right*!" laughed Harold. "And I thought *we* were con artists!"

George and Harold walked away chuckling. It was time to move on to bigger and better things.

CHAPTER 5

BIGGER AND BETTER THINGS

George and Harold went to the other end
of the gymnasium, opened their backpacks,
and began to work.

George busied himself by turning all
the spray nozzles on the *Automatic Dog
Washer* around, while Harold filled up the
soap tank with India ink.

Then they moved on to the *Volcano Detector*. "Will you please pass me the big bag of butterscotch pudding and a Phillips-head screwdriver?" asked Harold.

"Sure," said George, as he carefully inserted eggs into the *Electric Ping-Pong Ball Server*.

CHAPTER 6

THE INVENTION CONVENTION

The following day started out sunny and cheerful. The students and teachers filed into the gymnasium and checked their seats *very* carefully before sitting down.

"Greetings," said Mr Krupp, who was standing up at the microphone. "You don't need to worry about sticky seats today," he said. "I've taken measures to ensure that *this* Invention Convention won't be a disaster like *last* year's."

Everyone settled in as Madison Mancini, a third grader, stepped onstage to demonstrate her *Automatic Dog Washer*.

"First," said Madison, "you put your dog in the tub. Then you press this button."

Madison pressed the Start button. At first, nothing happened. Then, suddenly, a spurt of inky black water sprayed up

and out over the crowd. Everyone (except
the dog) got soaked, as Madison tried
desperately to turn off the sprayers.

"I can't stop it!" she cried. "Someone
turned all the nozzles around!"

"Now *who* could've done that?" asked
Mr Krupp.

Next up was Donny Shoemyer, with his Electric Ping-Pong Ball Server. He turned the machine on, and immediately it began hurling extra-large grade-A eggs into the crowd.

"Phoop!-Phoop!-Phoop!-Phoop!-Phoop!" went the machine.

"Splat!-Splat!-Splat!-Splat!-Splat!" went the eggs.

"I can't turn the machine off!" cried Donny. "Somebody jammed a paper clip into the controller!"

"Now *who* could've done that?" asked Ms Ribble.

Freddie Moore's Volcano Detector was also a big flop. When Freddie connected the circuits to the nine-volt battery, a large spring (which had been crammed into the centre of his miniature volcano) launched a giant plastic bag of butterscotch pudding high into the crowd.

It landed somewhere between the third and fourth rows. *Splat!*

"Hey!" whined Freddie. "Somebody put pudding in my volcano!"

"Now *who* could've done that?" asked Mr Meaner.

The rest of the day went on much the same way, with people shouting everything from "Hey! Who put oatmeal in my solar-powered leaf blower?" to "Hey, who let all the mice out of my treadmill dune buggy?"

It wasn't long before everyone fled the gymnasium, and the Second Annual Invention Convention had to be called off.

"How could this have happened?!!?" cried Mr Krupp as he wiped chocolate syrup, pencil shavings and cream-of-mushroom soup off his face and shirt. "George and Harold have been in study hall all day long! I put them there *myself*!"

"Um, excuse me, Mr Krupp," said Melvin Sneedly. "I think I have an answer to your question."

CHAPTER 7

BUSTED

CRASH! went the door to the study hall room. Mr Krupp stomped in like a crazy person. George and Harold had *never* seen him this upset before.

"You boys are in *SO* MUCH TROUBLE!" Mr Krupp shouted. "I'm putting you two on PERMANENT DETENTION for the REST OF THE SCHOOL YEAR!"

"Wait a second," cried George. "You can't prove anything!"

"Yeah," said Harold. "We've been here all day!"

Mr Krupp smiled devilishly, and looked toward the door. "Oh, *Melvin*," he called.

Melvin Sneedly stepped into the room, covered in mustard, eggshells and shredded coconut.

"They did it," Melvin said, pointing at George and Harold. "I saw 'em last night in the gym!"

"Melvin!" cried George, horrified. "You *promised*!"

"I changed my mind," Melvin said, grinning smugly. "Have fun in detention!"

CHAPTER 8

THE INVENTION CONVENTION DETENTION

After school, Mr Krupp ushered George and Harold into the detention room and wrote a long sentence on the chalkboard.

"From now on," growled Mr Krupp, "you boys will spend *two hours a day* after school copying this sentence over and over. I want every chalkboard in this room filled *completely*!"

On his way out of the door, Mr Krupp turned and said with an evil grin, "And if either of you leaves this room for *any* reason, I'm going to *suspend* you both!"

Now, as you might have guessed, writing sentences was nothing new to George and Harold. The two boys waited until Mr Krupp left the room, then they each took four homemade wooden rods out of their backpacks. The rods had holes in them that George and Harold had drilled in George's dad's workshop.

George screwed the rods together, while Harold inserted a piece of chalk into each hole.

Then they each took a pole and began
copying Mr Krupp's sentence. Every time
they wrote one sentence, the wooden poles
made twelve!

After about three and a half minutes,
every chalkboard in the room was completely
filled.

George and Harold sat down and admired their work.

"We've got a lot of time on our hands now," said George. "Got any ideas?"

"Let's make a new comic book!" said Harold.

So the two boys took out some paper and pens and created an all-new adventure about their favourite superhero. It was called *Captain Underpants and the Attack of the Talking Toilets*.

CHAPTER 10

A BIG MISTAKE

George and Harold sat together in the detention room, reading through their newest comic book and beaming proudly.

"We've got to go to the office and make copies of this," said George, "so we can sell them on the playground tomorrow."

"We can't," said Harold. "Don't you remember? Mr Krupp said he'd *suspend* us if he caught us leaving this room!"

"Then we won't let him catch us," said George.

George and Harold sneaked out of the
room quietly and crawled down the hall to
the office.

"Uh-oh," said Harold. "There's a bunch
of teachers in there. We'll never get to use
the copy machine."

"Hmmm," said George. "Are there any
other copy machines in this school?"

"How about the one that Melvin had in
the gym?" asked Harold.

"Oh, yeah," said George.

George and Harold crept over to the gym and found the PATSY 2000.

"I wonder if this machine still makes copies," said Harold. "Melvin *did* say that he had made some adjustments to it."

"Oh, he probably just crammed a mouse in there to fool us," said George. "It's the oldest trick in the book. I'm sure the machine still makes normal copies."

George placed the cover of their new comic book facedown on the glass screen and pressed Start.

All at once, the lights in the whole
school dimmed and the PATSY 2000 began
to shake and clunk around wildly. Giant
volts of static electricity zapped out the
bottom of the machine as a great whirl-
wind rose from the top. Loose papers and
other small objects in the room were
sucked into the wind, and they spun above
the machine like a raging cyclone.

"I don't think it's supposed to do this!"
shouted George over the horrible noise.

Finally, after a series of flashes and loud
zaps, the noise, wind and sparks stopped
altogether. The only sound that could be
heard was of something groaning and claw-
ing about inside the bloated, battered frame
of the PATSY 2000.

"It sounds like something's *alive* inside
there," said Harold.

George snatched the comic book from
the top of the machine. "Let's get out of
here!" he cried.

Just then, a small *ding* was heard and a full-sized, shiny white toilet emerged from the side of the PATSY 2000. Its teeth were sharp and jagged, and its angry eyeballs glowed with red, swelling veins. "YUM, YUM, EAT 'EM UP!" cried the evil toilet.

Almost immediately, another talking toilet emerged, followed by another, and another and *another*. "YUM, YUM, EAT 'EM UP!" they cried.

"Oh, *NO*! Melvin was *RIGHT*!!! The Photo-Atomic Trans-Somgobulating Yectofantriplutoniczanziptomiser really *DOES* create living, breathing, three-dimensional copies of one-dimensional images!" Harold cried convolutedly.

"I've got an idea," said George.

"What?" asked Harold.

"RUN!" cried George.

CHAPTER 11

THE INVENTION
CONVENTION
DETENTION SUSPENSION

George and Harold screamed and ran
through the gym door, closing it tightly
behind them.

"A-*HA*!!!" yelled Mr Krupp, who was just
coming down the hall. "You boys left the
detention room! You know what that
means, don't you?!!?"

"*It wasn't our fault!*" cried Harold.

"*Too* bad!" Mr Krupp shouted with
delight. "You boys are officially
SUSPENDED!!!"

"*Wait,*" cried George. "You've got to listen! Behind this door is an army of evil, vicious talk—"

"I don't have to listen to you boys *ever again,*" laughed Mr Krupp. "Now get your stuff and get out of this school!"

"But . . . but. . . ." Harold stammered, "you don't understa—"

"*GET OUT!!!*" Mr Krupp screamed.

George and Harold groaned and walked to their lockers to collect their stuff.

"Gosh," said Harold. "In one day we've had detention, suspension *and* we've created an army of evil talking toilets who want to take over the world."

"That's a pretty bad day, even by *our* standards," said George.

"Oh, well," said Harold. "I just hope things don't get any worse."

CHAPTER 12

THINGS GET WORSE

Word spread quickly throughout the office that George and Harold had been suspended. The teachers rushed out to cheer and laugh at the two boys.

"You're in big trouble now," chuckled Miss Anthrope. "I can't wait to call your parents and tell them the news!"

"Let's take their desks outside and chop them up!" cried Ms Ribble.

"Let's throw a party in the gym!" shouted Mr Meaner.

"*NOOO!*" cried George. "Whatever you do, *DON'T* open the door to the gym!"

"We can do whatever we like," snarled Mr Meaner as he dashed over to the gymnasium door. "Look, I'm opening the door!" He quickly opened the gym door. "Now I'm closing the door," he said.

"Now I'm opening the door again, and now I'm—*AAAAAAAAHH mmblemble* gluh!"

An evil toilet had stuck its mouth through the door, snapped Mr Meaner up, and swallowed him whole! *"Flusssssh!"*

The Talking Toilets then pushed their way through the open gymnasium doors and spilled out into the hallway.

"YUM, YUM, EAT 'EM UP!" the toilets bellowed. "YUM, YUM, EAT 'EM UP!"

The teachers couldn't believe their eyes. They screamed and ran for their lives. Only Mr Krupp, Ms Ribble, and George and Harold remained, frozen in fear. They watched, paralyzed, as the talking toilets came nearer and nearer. Finally, Ms Ribble pointed at the toilets and snapped her fingers.

"SNAP!"

"Go away," she cried. "Go away this minute!" But the toilets didn't listen. They moved closer and closer.

Finally, Ms Ribble turned and ran. Mr Krupp, however, just stood there in a daze. George and Harold looked up at him.

"Uh-oh," said Harold. "Did she just *snap her fingers*?!!?"

"Yep," said George. "Now we're *really* in trouble."

And George was right, for at that moment, Mr Krupp had begun to change. A silly, heroic smile came over his face as he stood defiantly before his foes.

"I'll put a stop to you vile villains," he said fearlessly. "But first, I need some *supplies*!!!"

Mr Krupp turned and dashed to his
office. George and Harold ran after him.

"Why did Ms Ribble have to snap her
fingers?!!?" cried George. *"Why?!!?"*

"Never mind that," cried George. "Mr
Krupp is turning into Captain Underpants!
We've got to pour water over his head
before it's too late!"

CHAPTER 13

IT'S TOO LATE!

When George and Harold reached Mr Krupp's office, they found only his clothes, shoes and toupee on the floor.

"Look," said Harold. "The window is open, and one of the red curtains is missing."

"What do we do now?" asked George. "Do we save Captain Underpants, or do we stay here and get eaten by a bunch of toilets?"

"Hmmm. . . Let me think about that one!" said Harold as he climbed out of the window.

George quickly collected Mr Krupp's
things and shoved them into his backpack.
Then he jumped out the window after
Harold. The two boys slid down the flagpole
and ran off after Captain Underpants.

"Where does he think he's going?" asked
George.

"I have *no* idea," said Harold. "But we'd
better run fast because I think we're being
followed!"

Captain Underpants dashed through the backyards of some nearby houses and collected pairs of underwear from the clotheslines.

"Mummy," said a little boy looking out his window, "a man in a red cape just stole our underwear."

HOW TO
LOSE 20
POUNDS
in 3 DAYS

"And now two boys are being chased by
a ferocious-looking toilet with sharp,
pointy teeth, screaming, 'Yum, yum, eat
'em up!'"

"Yeah, *right*!" laughed his mother. "Just
how *gullible* do you think I am?!!?"

CHAPTER 14

THE TALKING
TOILET TAKEOVER

When Captain Underpants had finished commandeering the underwear of local civilians, he dashed back to Jerome Horwitz Elementary to save the day.

The school was now overrun with chaos. Ms Ribble came tearing out of the door, followed by several evil toilets.

"Help me!" she cried. "They've swallowed every teacher in the whole building except me!"

"Don't worry, ma'am, I won't let them eat you up," Captain Underpants said, as a toilet ate her up.

"Oops!" said Captain Underpants.

Now, only George, Harold and Captain Underpants were left. They stood on the front lawn of the school, completely surrounded by hungry, drooling toilets.

"YUM, YUM, EAT 'EM UP!" the Talking Toilets chanted. "YUM, YUM, EAT 'EM UP! *YUM, YUM, EAT 'EM UP!* YUM, YUM, EAT 'EM UP!"

"We're *doomed*!" cried Harold.

"*Never* underestimate the power of underwear!" cried Captain Underpants, as he stretched and shot underwear into the waiting mouths of the Talking Toilets.

Unfortunately, the toilets just swallowed the underwear whole. It only seemed to make them hungrier and hungrier.

"If only we could think of something that would make them really *sick*," said George.

"Yeah," Harold continued. "Something so vile and disgusting, it would make them all *blow their guts* and writhe in agony!"

Suddenly, George and Harold's faces lit up. "CAFETERIA FOOD!" they shouted. And, faster than a speeding waistband, our three heroes dashed into the school.

CHAPTER 15

CREAMED MINCED BEEF TO THE RESCUE!

George, Harold and Captain Underpants got inside the school safely and closed the front door behind them. "I think the toilets are all outside," said George.

"But not for long," said Harold.

Quickly they ran to the school's kitchen and discovered a cart holding a large vat of something green and sludgy.

"Yuck," said George, holding his nose. "What *is* that stuff?"

"I think it's tomorrow's lunch," said Harold.

"Perfect!" said George. "I never thought I'd be *glad* to see creamed minced beef!"

Together, they wheeled the tub of stinky green glop down the hallway and through the side door of the school. Captain Underpants sat on the cart and stretched a pair of underwear over his head like a slingshot.

George stood over him, scooped some cafeteria food into the underwear, and stretched it back. Harold wheeled the cart towards the Talking Toilets.

"Tra-La-Laaaaaa!!!!" shouted Captain Underpants loudly.

The Talking Toilets turned and saw our three heroes. All at once, they shouted "YUM, YUM, EAT 'EM UP!" and the chase was on!

THOK!

Harold pulled the cart across the playground as the toilets zipped after them.

"Fire One!" cried Captain Underpants.

George shot a glob of creamed minced beef into the first toilet's mouth. The toilet swallowed it whole.

Harold kept pulling, as George scooped another serving into the underwear and pulled it back.

"Fire Two!" cried Captain Underpants.

Zip! went the cafeteria food, right into the *second* toilet's mouth.

The whole process repeated itself until every last toilet had swallowed at least two servings of creamed minced beef.

"We're almost out of ammo!" Captain Underpants shouted.

"And I don't think I can run any more," said Harold, huffing and puffing.

"Don't worry. . . *look*!" said George, pointing at the toilets.

They had all slowed down and were beginning to groan and wobble around. Their eyes crossed, and they turned an odd shade of green.

"Look out," cried Harold. "I think they're gonna *hurl*!"

And that's just what they did!

George, Harold and Captain Underpants watched as the toilets chucked up everything they had eaten during the day. The creamed minced beef, the underwear, even the teachers all came out without a scratch.

Then the toilets spun around in small circles and fell to the ground, dead.

George checked the teachers. "They're *alive*," he said. "*Unconscious*, but alive!"

"Wow," said Harold. "That was *easy*!"

"*Too* easy," said George.

"What do you mean?" asked Harold.

George pulled their comic book out of his backpack and showed it to Harold. "Remember how the PATSY 2000 turned everything on the front cover of our comic book to life?" he asked.

"Yeah, so?" said Harold.

"Well," said George, as he pointed to the *Turbo Toilet 2000* on the front cover of the comic. "We haven't seen *him* yet!"

CHAPTER 16

THE TURBO TOILET 2000

Suddenly, the Turbo Toilet 2000 came charging out of the front door of the school with a terrible *CRASH*! The earth rumbled beneath its mighty footsteps as nearly a ton of twisting steel and raging porcelain descended upon our heroes.

"You three meddling fools may have destroyed my army of Talking Toilets..." screamed the Turbo Toilet 2000, "...but you're *all out* of cafeteria food! How are you gonna stop *ME*?!!?"

"I'll tell you how," Captain Underpants said boldly. "With *Wedgie Power*!"

"*Wait*, Captain Underpants!" cried George. "You can't fight that thing! He'll rip you to pieces!"

"Boys," said Captain Underpants nobly, "I *must* fight valiantly for Truth, Justice and *all* that is Pre-Shrunk and Cottony!"

Captain Underpants leaped on to the Turbo Toilet 2000, and the battle began.

"I sure hope this doesn't lead to extremely graphic violence," said Harold.

"Me, too," said George.

CHAPTER 17

THE EXTREMELY GRAPHIC

VIOLENCE CHAPTER, PART 1

(IN FLIP-O-RAMA™)

WARNING:

The following chapter contains intense scenes showing a man in his underwear battling a giant toilet.

Please do not try this at home.

Introducing
FLIP-
In the past, literally dozens of epic novels have been written that have changed the course of history: *Moby Dick*, *Gone with the Wind*, and of course, *Captain Underpants and the Attack of the Talking Toilets!*
The only difference between our novel and those other "brand X" novels is that ours is the only one that cares enough to bring you the latest in "Cheesy Animation Technology!"
THE ART OF
FLiP-O-RAMA

PILKEY® BRAND
O-RAMA

HERE'S HOW IT WORKS!

Step 1
Place your *left* hand inside the dotted lines marked "LEFT HAND HERE". Hold the book open *flat*.

Step 2
Grasp the *right-hand* page with your right thumb and index finger (inside the dotted lines marked "RIGHT THUMB HERE").

Step 3
Now *quickly* flip the right-hand page back and forth until the picture appears to be *animated*.

(For extra fun, try adding your own sound-effects!)

FLIP-O-RAMA 1

(pages 219 and 221)

Remember, flip *only* page 219.
While you are flipping, be sure you
can see the picture on page 219
and the one on page 221.
If you flip quickly, the two
pictures will start to look like
one *animated* picture.

Don't forget to
add your own sound-effects!

LEFT HAND HERE

WEDGIE POWER
VS
POTTY POWER

RIGHT
THUMB
HERE

WEDGIE POWER
VS
POTTY POWER

FLIP-O-RAMA 2

(pages 223 and 225)

Remember, flip *only* page 223.
While you are flipping, be sure you
can see the picture on page 223
and the one on page 225.
If you flip quickly, the two
pictures will start to look like
one *animated* picture.

Don't forget to
add your own sound-effects!

LEFT HAND HERE

OH, *NO!!!*
THE POTTY POWER
PUNCH PREVAILS!

RIGHT
THUMB
HERE

RIGHT
INDEX
FINGER
HERE

OH, *NO!!!*
THE POTTY POWER
PUNCH PREVAILS!

FLIP-O-RAMA 3

(pages 227 and 229)

Remember, flip *only* page 227.
While you are flipping, be sure you
can see the picture on page 227
and the one on page 229.
If you flip quickly, the two
pictures will start to look like
one *animated* picture.

Don't forget to
add your own sound-effects!

LEFT HAND HERE

THE CARNIVOROUS
COMMODE
CAPTURES THE
CAPTAIN!

RIGHT
THUMB
HERE

RIGHT
INDEX
FINGER
HERE

THE CARNIVOROUS COMMODE CAPTURES THE CAPTAIN!

CHAPTER 18

HAROLD AND THE PURPLE
BALL-POINT PEN

Everything seemed hopeless. Captain
Underpants had slipped and fallen into
the mouth of the Turbo Toilet 2000, and
now the giant toilet was coming after
George and Harold!

"Ha, ha, ha, ha, ha!" laughed the
powerful porcelain predator. "Once I have
eaten you two kids up, I will *take over
the world*!"

"Not if *we* have
anything to say
about it!"
yelled George.

George and Harold ran into the school and locked the door behind them. The Turbo Toilet 2000 banged against the door with its fists, shouting, "You boys can't hide in there for ever!"

George and Harold ran to the gym.

"I've got a plan," said George. "We need to invent a character who can defeat a giant robot toilet."

"How about a giant robot urinal?" asked Harold. "We can call it *The Urinator*!"

"No way!" said George. "They'll never let us get away with that in a children's book. We're skating on *thin ice* as it is!"

"All right," said Harold, "how about a giant 'Plunger' robot? He can carry a really big plunger, and—"

"That's it!" cried George.

So Harold took out his purple ball-point pen and began to draw.

"Give him *laser* eyes," said George.

"All right," said Harold.

"And give him turbo-atomic rocket boosters," said George.

"Got it," said Harold.

"And make him obey our every command," said George.

"I'm *way* ahead of you," said Harold.

Harold finished his drawing, and George inspected it carefully.

"This just *might* work," said George.

"Yeah," said Harold. "If the PATSY 2000 can hold out."

The boys turned and looked at the dented, cracked and beaten-up machine laying on its side in the corner. George and Harold pushed the PATSY 2000 upright and dusted it off.

"Come on, PATSY, old girl," said George. "We really need you now!"

"Yeah," said Harold. "The fate of the entire planet is in our hands!"

CHAPTER 19

THE INCREDIBLE
ROBO-PLUNGER

George took Harold's picture and placed it on the screen of the PATSY 2000 and pressed Start.

The lights around them dimmed as the weary machine began to shake and smoke. Lightning bolts zapped, thunder clapped, and the whole gymnasium shook with Photo-Atomic Trans-Somgobulatory Yectofantriplutoniczanziptic energy.

"C'mon, PATSY!" George shouted over the horrible noise. "You can do it, baby!"

Finally a small *ding* was heard, and the PATSY 2000 coughed up a huge, metallic behemoth. It rose up and stood valiantly before George and Harold. It was the Incredible *Robo-Plunger*.

"*Hooray!*" cried George. "It *worked*!"

"Way to go, PATSY!" Harold cheered. "Now let's get outside and kick some Turbo Toilet Tushy!"

CHAPTER 20

THE EXTREMELY GRAPHIC VIOLENCE CHAPTER, PART 2 (IN FLIP-O-RAMA™)

NOTICE:

The following chapter contains terribly naughty scenes depicting a giant toilet getting kicked where it's shiny.

All toilet violence was carefully monitored by PETT (People for the Ethical Treatment of Toilets).

No actual toilets were harmed during the making of this chapter.

FLIP-O-RAMA 4

(pages 239 and 241)

Remember, flip *only* page 239.
While you are flipping, be sure you
can see the picture on page 239
and the one on page 241.
If you flip quickly, the two
pictures will start to look like
one *animated* picture.

Don't forget to
add your own sound-effects!

LEFT HAND HERE

THE INCREDIBLE ROBO-PLUNGER TO THE RESCUE!

RIGHT THUMB HERE

RIGHT
INDEX
FINGER
HERE

THE INCREDIBLE ROBO-PLUNGER TO THE RESCUE!

FLIP-O-RAMA 5

(pages 243 and 245)

Remember, flip *only* page 243.
While you are flipping, be sure you
can see the picture on page 243
and the one on page 245.
If you flip quickly, the two
pictures will start to look like
one *animated* picture.

Don't forget to
add your own sound-effects!

LEFT HAND HERE

THE INCREDIBLE ROBO-PLUNGER KICKS THE TT 2000'S TUSHY!

243

RIGHT
THUMB
HERE

RIGHT
INDEX
FINGER
HERE

ROBO-PLUNGER KICKS THE TT 2000'S TUSHY!

FLIP-O-RAMA 6

(pages 247 and 249)

Remember, flip *only* page 247.
While you are flipping, be sure you
can see the picture on page 247
and the one on page 249.
If you flip quickly, the two
pictures will start to look like
one *animated* picture.

Don't forget to
add your own sound-effects!

LEFT HAND HERE

THE TT 2000
TAKES
THE PLUNGE!

RIGHT
THUM
HERE

RIGHT
INDEX
FINGER
HERE

THE TT 2000
TAKES
THE PLUNGE!

CHAPTER 21

THE AFTERMATH

The Incredible Robo-Plunger had defeated the evil Turbo Toilet 2000, but George and Harold's problems weren't over yet. They reached into the crumpled mouth of the TT 2000 and pulled out their principal.

"What happened here?" cried Mr Krupp. "The school has been *destroyed*, the teachers are all *unconscious,* and I'm standing here in my *underwear*!"

"Uh-oh!" Harold whispered. "Captain Underpants must have got toilet water on his head. He's turned back into Principal Krupp!"

George took Mr Krupp's clothes and hair out of his backpack and handed them to him.

"I'm ruined!" Principal Krupp whined as he dressed himself. "I'm going to be held responsible for this mess! I'm going to lose my job!"

"Maybe not," said George. "We can fix everything, and clean up this whole mess."

"Yeah," said Harold, "but it'll cost you!"

"Cost me *what*?" asked Mr Krupp.

"Well," said George, "we'd like you to cancel our detention *and* our suspension!"

"And we'd also like to be *Principals for the Day*!" said Harold.

"All right," said Mr Krupp. "If you can really fix *everything*, you've got a deal!"

George and Harold turned and spoke to
the Incredible Robo-Plunger.

"All right, robot guy," said George,
"make yourself useful and pick up all this
mess!"

"Yeah, and fix up the school, too," said
Harold. "Use your laser eyes to repair all
the broken windows and stuff!"

"And when you're done," said George,
"take all the evidence, and fly it up to
Uranus."

"And don't come back!" said Harold.

CHAPTER 22

TO MAKE A LONG

STORY SHORT

The robot obeyed.

CHAPTER 23
AFTER THE AFTERMATH

The Incredible Robo-Plunger soared off into space just as the teachers began to regain consciousness.

"I just had the strangest dream," said Ms Ribble. "It was all about these evil toilets who wanted to take over the world."

"We had the same dream, too," said the other teachers.

"Well," said Mr Krupp, "things turned out all right after all!"

"Not quite," said George. "It's *payback* time!"

CHAPTER 24

PRINCIPALS FOR THE DAY

(OR, THE INVENTION CONVENTION DETENTION SUSPENSION PREVENTION)

"Attention, students," said George over the intercom the following day. "This is Principal George. You are all excused from classes today. There will be no homework or tests, and everybody gets an *A+* for the day."

"That's right," said Principal Harold. "Also, we are hosting an all-day breaktime outside, complete with free pizza, French fries, cotton candy and a live DJ. Now go outside and play."

Principal George and Principal Harold strolled out to the playground to behold their glorious domain. George got a slice of pepperoni pizza, while Harold made himself a banana split at the all-you-can-eat ice-cream sundae bar.

"It's *good* to be the principal!" said
George.

"Yep," said Harold. "I wish we could be
principals every day!"

PIQUA
PIZZA
PALACE

Later, George and Harold paid a visit to the unfortunate folks who were spending the day writing sentences in the detention room. All the teachers were there, along with Mr Krupp and Melvin Sneedly.

Mr Krupp looked out of the window at the all-day breaktime celebration going on outside.

"How are you boys going to *pay* for all that ice cream and pizza?" he asked.

"Oh, we sold some stuff," said Harold.

"What did you sell?" asked Mr Krupp.

"Your antique walnut desk and leather chair," said George. "And all the furniture in the teachers' lounge."

"WHAT?!!?" screamed Mr Krupp.

"Umm . . . I think we'd better leave now," said Harold.

George and Harold left the detention
room in a hurry. Miss Anthrope snapped
her fingers at them.

Snap!

"Come back here right now!" she yelled.
"Uh-oh," said George. "Did Miss
Anthrope just *snap her fingers*?"

Within seconds, Mr Krupp dashed out of the detention room and ran down the hall-way towards his office. He had a goofy, heroic, *all-too-familiar-looking* smile on his face.

"Oh, no!" cried Harold.
"Here we go *again*!" said George.

FOR JOHN "SPARKY" JOHNSON

CHAPTERS

Hello . . . it's us again! Before you read this book, there's some things you should know . . . So Harold and I have created this informative pamphlet to fill you in on the details.
Please don't let this comic fall into the wrong hands.

This has been A public servise
Anouncement from George and Harold...
Who STILL Deny everyThing!

CHAPTER 1

GEORGE AND HAROLD

This is George Beard and Harold Hutchins.
George is the kid on the left with the tie
and the flat-top. Harold is the one on the
right with the T-shirt and the bad haircut.
Remember that now.

If you were looking for a few words to describe George and Harold, you might come up with *kind, funny, smart, determined* and *deep.*

Just ask their principal, Mr Krupp. He'll tell you that George and Harold are **KIND**a **FUNNY**-lookin' **SMART** alecks who are **DETERMINED** to drive everybody off the **DEEP** end!

But don't listen to him.

George and Harold are actually very clever and good-hearted boys. Their only problem is that they're fourth graders. And at George and Harold's school, fourth graders are expected to sit still and pay attention for *seven hours a day*!

George and Harold are just not very good at that.

The only thing George and Harold *are* good at is being silly. Unfortunately, George and Harold's silliness gets them into trouble every now and then. Sometimes it gets them into a LOT of trouble. And one time it got them into *SO MUCH* trouble, it almost caused the entire Earth to be destroyed by an army of giant evil zombie nerds!

But before I can tell you that story, I have to tell you *this* story....

CHAPTER 2

THE EVIL SPACE GUYS

One dark, clear night in Piqua, Ohio,
a flaming object was seen streaking across
the quiet midnight sky.

It shone brightly for a second or two,
then fizzled out just above Jerome Horwitz
Elementary School. Nobody gave it a
second thought.

The next day, everything seemed pretty normal. Nobody noticed anything different about the school. Nobody paid any attention to the roof. And of course, nobody looked up and said, "Hey, what's that big spaceship thingy doing on the roof of the school?"

Perhaps if they had, the horrible ordeal that followed might never have happened, and you wouldn't be sitting here reading about it right now. But they didn't, it did, and, well, here we are.

As we can all plainly see, there was a spaceship on top of the building. And inside that spaceship were three of the most evil, hideous, and merciless space-men ever to set foot on the roof of a small midwestern elementary school.

Their names were Zorx, Klax and Jennifer. Their mission? To take over planet Earth.

"First," said Zorx, "we must find a way to infiltrate the school."

"Then," said Klax, "we will turn all the children into giant, super-powered evil zombie nerds!"

"Finally," said Jennifer, "we will use them to take over the world!"

Zorx and Klax laughed and laughed.

"Silence, you fools!" barked Jennifer. "If our plan is to work, we must wait until it is narratively convenient. In the meantime, we will watch their every move on our trinocloscope!"

CHAPTER 3

FUN WITH SCIENCE

Early that same morning, George and Harold were sitting in their 10:15 AM science class making silly noises.

"Meeowwwww," George mewed softly, without moving his lips.

"Rrrr-rrr-rrrr," growled Harold, without opening his mouth.

"There it is *again*!" exclaimed their science teacher, Mr Fyde. "I *distinctly* heard a cat and a dog in here!"

"We didn't hear anything," the children said, trying not to laugh.

"I-I must be *hearing* things again," Mr Fyde worried.

"Maybe you should leave and go and see a doctor," said George with concern.

"I can't," said Mr Fyde. "Today is the day of the *big volcano experiment*."

The children all groaned. Mr Fyde's science experiments were usually the most idiotic things on earth. They almost never worked, and were *always* boring.

But today's experiment was different. Mr Fyde brought in a large, fake-looking volcano that he had made out of papier-mâché. He filled the volcano with a box of ordinary baking soda.

"Baking soda is also called 'sodium bicarbonate'," explained Mr Fyde.

"Meeeeowwwwwww."

"Umm…" said Mr Fyde, "did any of you children just hear – umm, uh … never mind."

Mr Fyde opened up a bottle of clear liquid. "Now watch what happens when I pour vinegar on to the baking soda," he said.

The children watched as the tiny volcano started to rumble. Soon, a large glob of foamy goop spurted out the top. The goop poured over the desk and dripped on to the floor, creating a huge mess.

"Oops," said Mr Fyde. "I guess I used too much baking soda."

George and Harold were stunned.

"How did you do that?" asked Harold.

"Well," said Mr Fyde, "the vinegar acts as a liberating agent, which releases the gaseous carbonate radical element of the sodium bicarbo—"

"Meeeeooowwwwwwww."

"Umm … uh," Mr Fyde paused. "Uh, e-excuse me, children. I-I've got to go and see a doctor."

Mr Fyde put on his coat and hurried
through the door. George and Harold
got up and studied the messy volcano
experiment with great interest.

"Are you thinking what I'm thinking?"
asked George.

"I think I'm thinking what you're
thinking," said Harold.

CHAPTER 4

THE SETUP

After school, the two boys raced to George's house and got down to business.

George and Harold sat down and began creating a fake cupcake recipe.

"We'll just add a box of baking soda and a bottle of vinegar to this recipe," said George. "And whoever makes these cupcakes will get a big surprise!"

"Let's add *two* boxes of baking soda and *two* bottles of vinegar to the recipe," said Harold. "That way, they'll get an even *bigger* surprise!"

"Good idea!" laughed George.

CHAPTER 5

MR KRUPP'S KRISPY KRUPCAKES

The next morning at school, George and Harold strolled into the cafeteria and taped a festive-looking card to the kitchen door.

KITCHEN

LUNCH
LADYS

Soon the lunch ladies arrived.

"Oh, look," said Miss Creant, the head lunch lady. "Today is Mr Krupp's birthday and he'd like us to make a batch of cupcakes just for him! Isn't that cute?"

"I've got an idea," said the cook, Mrs DePoint. "Why don't we surprise him and make cupcakes for the *whole school*!"

"Good thinking," said Miss Creant. "Let's see now ... this recipe serves ten, and we have about 1,000 students and teachers in the school, so...

...we'll need 100 eggs, 150 cups of flour, 200 boxes of baking soda, 7 quarts of green food colouring, 50 sticks of butter, 150 cups of sugar — and, let's see... Oh yes, 200 bottles of *vinegar*!"

MR. KRUPP'S KRISPY KRUPCAKES

INGREDIENTS

1 egg
1½ cups of Flour
2 Boxes BAKING Soda
1¼ cups SugAR
1 Stick Butter
Green Food coleRing
2 Bottles VinegAR

MAKES 10 cupcAKes

DIRECTIONS

Mix Flour And SugAR with baking Soda, and egg. Melt butter, Pour into Mixture. Stir in Food coleRing. Now Add VinegAR. Mix well. Pour into cupcAKe Thingies. Bake At 45 degrees For 3 hours.

The lunch ladies scurried about, gathering everything they needed. They dumped the eggs, food colouring, milk and baking soda into a large vat and began to mix thoroughly.

Then somebody poured in the vinegar...

CHAPTER 6

WHAT HAPPENED NEXT

(Note: Please shake this book back and forth uncontrollably when you read the following word. Also, shout it out as loud as you can. Don't worry, you won't get in trouble.)

"KA-BLOOOOOSH!"

CHAPTER 6 ¹/₂

HERE COMES THE GOOP!

A giant wave of green goop crashed through
the cafeteria doors and splashed down the
halls, swallowing everything in its path.
Book bags, bulletin boards, lunch boxes,
coat racks, trophy cases ... nothing could
stand in the way of the gigantic green
glob o' goo.

It travelled down the north, east and
west wings of the school, covering everything from the drinking fountains to the
text on this page. It squished into lockers,
and squashed down the stairs. It billowed
int⸻ ⸻and ball⸻

It wasn't long before the green goop
began spilling into all the classrooms.

"Uh-oh," said George. "Something tells
me the lunch ladies made more than just
one batch of Mr Krupp's Krispy Krupcakes."

"But – but that was *their* idea, not
ours," cried Harold.

"Speaking of *ideas*," said George, "I've
got a good one."

"What?" asked Harold.

"*RUN!*" cried George.

CHAPTER 7

THE WRATH OF THE CAFETERIA LADIES

The next afternoon, as cleaning crews sorted through the sticky green hallways and sticky green classrooms, the cafeteria ladies had a meeting with Mr Krupp in his sticky green office.

"But it wasn't even my birthday!" cried Mr Krupp.

"We know you had nothing to do with this!" said Miss Creant. "We think it was those two awful boys, George and Harold!"

"Well, *duh!*" said Mr Krupp, rolling his eyes. "OF COURSE IT WAS GEORGE AND HAROLD!!! But do you have any proof?"

"PROOF?!!?" said the lunch ladies. "Why, George and Harold are *always* playing tricks on us! Every day, they change the letters around on our lunch sign. They put pepper in the napkin dispensers and unscrew the caps on the saltshakers... They start food fights... They go sledging on our lunch trays... They make everybody laugh so the milk squirts out of their noses... And they're *constantly creating these awful comic books about us*!!!"

CHAPTER 8

CAPTAIN UNDERPANTS AND THE NIGHT OF THE LIVING LUNCH LADIES

R.I.P.

By George Beard
and Harold Hutchins.

CAPTAIN UNDERPANTS and the NIGHT OF THE LIVING
LUNCH LADYS
STORY BY George Beard
Pictures By Harold Hutchins
Late one friday After noon, The Lunch Ladys were Cleaning up The caffeteria.
There's Lots of half-eaten Food in This TRASH Barrel.
Well pour it in and we'll Serve it again next week!
TRASH
STEW
Waste not want Not!
TRASH
STEW
But while they were Working, The janitor Axidentally Locked The School for The weekend.
closed
The Lunch Ladys were TRAPPED inside!
HELP!
They were forsed to eat there own Food To Survive.
Past The Lips
And over The gums..
Look out Tummy... Here it comes.

HelP! The Lunch Lady's ARosed From The dead! They're Hungry For brAinS And They just attacked the gym teacher.
But I thought you SAid They were hungry for "BrAins"?
PRINCIPLE
This Look s Like A job For...
CRASh
CAPTAIN UNderPAnTS!
what seems To Be The problem?
Living DEAD Lunch LAdys!
P
Don't worry--- I'll give Them wedgies!
OH No! wedgie Power doesn't work on The Living Dead!

CHAPTER 9

QUITTIN' TIME

"We're *fed up* with those two boys!" cried Miss Creant. "They're always making fun of our cooking!"

"Yeah!" said Mrs DePoint. "Our food isn't *that* bad. I ate here once and hardly got sick at all!"

"Well, I can't punish them if we don't have any proof," said Mr Krupp.

"Fine!" said the lunch ladies. "Then we *quit*!"

"Ladies, ladies," cried Mr Krupp. "Be reasonable! You can't just *quit* on such short notice."

But the lunch ladies didn't care. They marched right out of Mr Krupp's sticky green office, and that was the end of that.

"Rats!" cried Mr Krupp. "Now where am I going to find three new lunch ladies by tomorrow morning?"

Suddenly there was a knock on Mr Krupp's door. Three very large women wearing *lots* of make-up walked into his office.

"Hello," said the first woman. "My name is, uh, Zorx*ette*. These are my, uh, sisters, *Klaxette* and, umm, *Jenniferette*. We've come to apply for jobs as cafeteria ladies."

"Wow," said Mr Krupp. "Do you have any experience?"

"No," said Klaxette.

"Do you have any credentials?" asked Mr Krupp.

"No," said Zorxette.

"Do you have any references?" asked Mr Krupp.

"No," said Jenniferette.

"You're hired!" said Mr Krupp.

"Wonderful," said Jenniferette. "Now our plan to take over the world is – er, I mean, our plan to *feed the children healthy, nutritional meals* is underway!"

The three new lunch ladies laughed horribly. Then they left Mr Krupp's office and got started preparing the next day's lunch menu.

"Well, *that* was easy," said Mr Krupp.
"Now to take care of George and Harold!"

CHAPTER 10

BUSTED!

George and Harold were in study hall when they heard the dreaded announcement over the intercom:

> **"George Beard and Harold Hutchins, please report to Mr Krupp's office immediately."**

"Oh, no," cried Harold. "We're busted!"
"No way!" said George. "Remember, what happened yesterday was *not our fault*! We didn't do it – it was an *accident*!"

But Mr Krupp was not as understanding. "I can't prove it, but I *know* you boys are responsible for yesterday's disaster," Mr Krupp said. "I'm going to punish you by taking away your cafeteria privileges for the rest of the year! *No more cafeteria food for you two!*"

"No more cafeteria food?" whispered Harold, "I thought he said he was going to *punish* us."

"Yeah." George smiled. "Maybe if we're *really* bad, he'll take away our *homework* privileges, too!"

"I heard that!" screamed Mr Krupp. "From now on, you boys are going to have to pack your own lunches and eat them in my office so I can keep an eye on you!"

"Rats!" said Harold.

"But we didn't do it!" George protested. "WE DIDN'T DO IT!"

"Too bad!" said Mr Krupp.

"Boy," said George. "This is probably
the first time we've got in trouble for something we *didn't* do."

"Unless you count all those times we
didn't do our homework," said Harold.

"Oh, yeah," laughed George.

CHAPTER 11

BROWN BAGGIN' IT

The next day, George and Harold each brought their own sandwiches to Mr Krupp's office for lunch.

"I'll trade you half of my peanut-butter-and-gummy-worm sandwich," said George, "for half of your tuna-salad-with-chocolate-chips-and-miniature-marshmallows sandwich."

"Sure," said Harold. "Y'want some barbecue sauce on that?"

"You kids are DISGUSTING!" Mr Krupp shouted.

Soon George and Harold were munching on potato chips with whipped cream and chocolate sprinkles. Mr Krupp was turning green.

"What's for dessert?" asked Harold.

"Hard-boiled eggs dipped in hot fudge and Skittles!" said George.

"AAAUGH!" screamed Mr Krupp. *"I can't stand it any more!"* He got up and stumbled through the door for some fresh air.

"You know," said George. "Now that Mr Krupp is gone, we could run to the cafeteria and change the letters around on the lunch sign."

"Cool," said Harold.

POTATO CHIPS

So George and Harold sneaked to the cafeteria. But when they read the lunch sign, they were a bit confused.

"What's going on here?" said George.

"It looks like somebody's already changed the sign," said Harold.

"Forget the sign," said George. "Look at everybody! *They've* changed!"

It was true. All the kids and teachers in school were entering the cafeteria looking as normal as ever. But they were leaving the cafeteria looking quite different.

"Look!" cried George. "They're all wearing broken eyeglasses held together with masking tape ... and they've all got vinyl pocket protectors!!! They've all turned into—"

"*Nerds!*" Harold gasped.

"And look at their skin," said George. "They're all grey and clammy. This can only mean one thing!"

"They're — they're ZOMBIE nerds?!!?" asked Harold.

"I'm afraid so," said George.

"Let's just hope they're friendly!" said Harold.

"Whoever heard of a *friendly* zombie nerd?" asked George.

"I'm afraid," Harold whined.

"There's no time to be afraid," said George. "We've got to get to the bottom of this!"

"*That's* what I'm afraid of," said Harold.

326

CHAPTER 12

THE BOTTOM OF THIS

George and Harold crawled into the
cafeteria and sneaked through the kitchen
doors. There they hid behind a table while
the incredibly naughty cafeteria ladies from
outer space discussed their plans to take
over the world.

"Look at those puny earthlings!" laughed Zorx. "They're all drinking Evil Zombie Nerd Milkshakes and transforming before our very eyes!"

"It won't be long now," said Klax. "Tomorrow, we'll feed them Super Evil Rapid-Growth Juice! Then they will grow to the size of Xleqxisfp trees."

"Exactly," sneered Jennifer. "Then we will unleash our giant evil zombie nerds upon the earth, and soon the planet will be OURS!"

The three evil space guys threw back their heads and laughed hysterically.

"We've got to tell Mr Krupp about this," Harold whispered.

"Right," whispered George. "But first, we've got to get rid of that SUPER EVIL RAPID-GROWTH JUICE!"

George carefully reached up and swiped the carton of juice.

"What should we do with it?" asked Harold.

"Let's pour it out of the window," said George. "That way it won't do any damage."

"Good idea," said Harold.

While the naughty cafeteria ladies continued laughing, George quietly emptied the carton of SUPER EVIL RAPID-GROWTH JUICE out of the window.

"You know," whispered Harold, "Mr Krupp is never going to believe that sinister cafeteria ladies from outer space have turned everybody into evil zombie nerds."

"Sure he'll believe us – he's GOT to believe us!" said George. "I *hope* he believes us!"

CHAPTER 13

HE DOESN'T BELIEVE THEM

"That's the most *ridiculous* story I've ever heard!" laughed Mr Krupp.

"But it's true!" cried Harold.

"Yeah," said George. "Everybody in the entire school is an evil zombie nerd! The kids, the teachers ... *everybody*!"

"All right," said Mr Krupp. "I'll prove it to you!" He pressed the button on his intercom and called for his secretary.

Soon Miss Anthrope entered the room. She was dressed in a pink polka-dot polyester dress, with orthopedic knee-high stockings and ugly brown arch-support loafers.

"*See?*" said Harold. "She's dressed like a *nerd*!"

"She *always* dresses like that," snapped Mr Krupp.

"But she's grey and clammy and reeks of *freakish zombified death*!" cried George.

"She *always smells like that*!" Mr Krupp argued. "And she's always grey and clammy, too!"

George and Harold had to admit that school secretaries were not very good subjects to compare and contrast with evil zombie nerds.

But then, Miss Anthrope leaned over and took a huge bite out of Mr Krupp's desk. *"Must destroy Earth,"* she moaned as she took another bite.

Even Mr Krupp had to agree that Miss Anthrope was acting a bit more evil than usual.

MUNCH
MUNCH

So George and Harold took Mr Krupp down to the cafeteria to confront the evil lunch ladies.

Suddenly, out of the shadows stepped the evil Zorx. "Gotcha!" Zorx cried, as he grabbed on to Harold's shoulders.

"Aaaagh!" screamed Harold. He squirmed away, pulling Zorx's gloves off and revealing two slimy green tentacles.

"See, Mr Krupp?" said George. "We told you they were space guys!"

"You FOOLS!" screamed Zorx. "Now we
will destroy you!" The evil Zorx pointed his
tentacle at George, Harold and Mr Krupp,
and snapped his fingers:

"SNAP!"

Suddenly, Mr Krupp began to change.

335

A heroic grin spread across Mr Krupp's
face. He threw out his chest and placed
his fists firmly at his sides, looking quite
triumphant.

"Uh-oh," said George. "That evil space
guy just snapped his fingers! Now Mr Krupp
is turning into *you-know-who*!"

"Hey, wait a second," said Harold.
"Tentacles don't have fingers! You can't
snap a tentacle!"

"There's no time to argue the physical
improbabilities of this story," said George.
"We've got to stop Mr Krupp from
changing into Captain Underpants before
it's too late!"

CHAPTER 14

IT'S TOO LATE

Mr Krupp turned and dashed out the door. His clothes flew off behind him as the hallways echoed with jubilant proclamations about the superiority of underwear.

George and Harold dashed after him, but
the door was quickly blocked by Zorx, Klax
and Jennifer.

"You wanna get out of this kitchen," the
evil Jennifer mocked, "you gotta go through
US!"

George grabbed a rolling pin. Harold
grabbed a cast-iron frying pan.

"I sure hope we don't have to resort to
incredibly graphic violence," said Harold.

"Me, too," said George.

CHAPTER 15

THE INCREDIBLY GRAPHIC VIOLENCE CHAPTER, PART 1 (IN FLIP-O-RAMA™)

WARNING:

The following chapter contains terribly inappropriate scenes that certainly do not belong in a children's book.

If you are offended by such senselessness, please put this book down immediately, raise your arms over your head, and run screaming to your nearest shoe shop. When you get there, ask them to make you a cheeseburger.

(Note: This probably won't help you a bit, but we think it will be funny.)

Introducing
FLIP:
Lately there have been many ground-breaking advances in the field of animation: there's claymation, dynamation, Japanese anime, and even computer animation!
But if you ask us, nothing beats the "economy-sized" thrills CHEESY ANIMATION TECHNOLOGY (also known as...)
FLIP-O-RAMA

PILKEY® BRAND
D·RAMA

HERE'S HOW IT WORKS!

STEP 1

Place your *left* hand inside the dotted lines marked "LEFT HAND HERE." Hold the book open *flat*.

STEP 2

Grasp the *right-hand* page with your right thumb and index finger (inside the dotted lines marked "RIGHT THUMB HERE").

STEP 3

Now *quickly* flip the right-hand page back and forth until the picture appears to be *animated*.

(For extra fun, try adding your own sound-effects!)

FLIP-O-RAMA 1

(pages 343 and 345)

Remember, flip *only* page 343.
While you are flipping, be sure you
can see the picture on page 343
and the one on page 345.
If you flip quickly, the two
pictures will start to look like
<u>one</u> *animated* picture.

Don't forget to
add your own sound-effects!

LEFT HAND HERE

GEORGE PINS
A PREDATOR

RIGHT
THUMB
HERE

RIGHT
INDEX
FINGER
HERE

GEORGE PINS
A PREDATOR

FLIP-O-RAMA 2

(pages 347 and 349)

Remember, flip *only* page 347.
While you are flipping, be sure you
can see the picture on page 347
and the one on page 349.
If you flip quickly, the two
pictures will start to look like
<u>one</u> *animated* picture.

Don't forget to
add your own sound-effects!

LEFT HAND HERE

HAROLD BONKS
A BAD GUY

RIGHT
THUMB
HERE

HAROLD BONKS
A BAD GUY

FLIP-O-RAMA 3

(pages 351 and 353)

Remember, flip *only* page 351.
While you are flipping, be sure you
can see the picture on page 351
and the one on page 353.
If you flip quickly, the two
pictures will start to look like
<u>one</u> *animated* picture.

Don't forget to
add your own sound-effects!

LEFT HAND HERE

GEORGE AND HAROLD
SAVE THE DAY
(FOR NOW)

RIGHT
THUMB
HERE

GEORGE AND HAROLD
SAVE THE DAY
(FOR NOW)

CHAPTER 16

THE ASSAULT OF THE EQUALLY EVIL LUNCHROOM ZOMBIE NERDS

George and Harold had barely caught their breath when Captain Underpants finally showed up.

"Tra-La-Laaaaa!" he said. "I'm here to fight for Truth, Justice and *all* that is Pre-Shrunk and Cottony!"

"Where were you back in chapter fifteen when we needed you?" asked George.

"I was at the shoe shop ordering a cheeseburger," said Captain Underpants.

While our three heroes were talking, nobody noticed that Zorx, Klax and Jennifer had slithered away. The wounded space guys approached the lunchroom loudspeakers and called for their evil zombie nerds.

"Zombie Nerds!" instructed Jennifer. "Destroy Captain Underpants – and his little friends, too!"

Soon, every evil zombie nerd in the entire school put down their *Omni* magazines and headed for the cafeteria.

"Must destroy Underpants," they
groaned. *"Must destroy Underpants!"*

Suddenly, our three heroes were
surrounded by evil, vicious zombie nerds.
Closer and closer they came.

"Oh, no!" cried George. "What do we do
now?"

"To the Underwear Cave!" shouted
Captain Underpants.

"There *is* no *Underwear Cave!*" said
Harold.

"Really?" said Captain Underpants. "Well,
let's just climb up that ladder instead."

George, Harold and Captain Underpants
scurried up the ladder, and soon they were
all on the roof.

"Well, we're safe now," said Harold.

"Yep," said George.

"That's for sure," said Captain
Underpants.

CHAPTER 17

OH YEAH?

It didn't take long before George, Harold, and Captain Underpants looked behind them.

"Hey," said Harold. "What's that big spaceship thingy doing on the roof of the school?"

"And where did that *super-evil rapidly growing* dandelion come from?" asked Captain Underpants.

George and Harold gasped. They looked at each other with the sudden panicked realization that only children who have accidentally created a giant mutated garden nuisance would know.

"Er…" stammered George. "We have *no idea* how *that* happened."

"Er… *Yeah*," said Harold. "Absolutely *no idea* at all!"

At that moment, the door to the roof swung open. Zorx poked his evil head out and shouted, "We've got you now!"

With nowhere else to run, our three heroes quickly scurried up the ladder of the big spaceship thingy and closed the door behind them.

Inside the spaceship, George, Harold and Captain Underpants discovered a refrigerator filled with strange juices.

"Look," said George. "Here's a carton of ANTI-EVIL-ZOMBIE-NERD JUICE. How convenient!"

"And look at this," said Harold. "A carton of ULTRA NASTY SELF-DESTRUCT JUICE. Now *this* could come in handy!"

"And look what I've found," said Captain Underpants. "A whole carton of EXTRA-STRENGTH SUPER POWER JUICE!"

"Hey, gimme that!" said George, snapping the carton out of Captain Underpants's hands.

362

CHAPTER 18

SPACE SLAVES

Suddenly, the door of the spaceship swung open, and the three evil space guys slithered inside.

"Step away from the refrigerator!" screamed Jennifer. "And get into that jail cell!"

George and Harold hid their juice cartons behind their backs, and our three heroes stepped quickly into the jail cell.

Zorx started up the engines and the spaceship lifted off. It rose a hundred metres in the air and hovered over the school.

"You three puny earthlings are very fortunate," said Jennifer. "You will get to witness the destruction of your planet from the safety of your jail cell. Afterwards, you will have the honour of being our obedient space slaves!"

"Aw, *man*!" said George and Harold.

"Quickly, Klax," said Jennifer. "Get me a carton of SUPER EVIL RAPID-GROWTH JUICE from the refrigerator. We can pour it into our spray gun and shower it upon our evil zombie nerds!"

CHAPTER 19

THE BIG SWITCHEROO

Klax returned with a carton of SUPER EVIL
RAPID-GROWTH JUICE, and placed it on the
control panel.

"*Soon,*" said Jennifer, "Earth will be
OURS!"

The three aliens threw back their heads
and laughed and laughed.

Suddenly, George got an idea.

He whispered to Harold for a second or two, then he quietly reached through the bars of the jail cell and swiped Klax's carton of SUPER EVIL RAPID-GROWTH JUICE.

George carefully peeled the label off the
carton, and stuck it over the label of his
ULTRA NASTY SELF-DESTRUCT JUICE.

While he was busy doing that, Harold
reached through the bars and switched the
labels of the SPRAY GUN and the FUEL TANK.

Finally, George reached back through the bars and put his carton of ULTRA NASTY SELF-DESTRUCT JUICE (which now read SUPER EVIL RAPID-GROWTH JUICE) on the control panel.

"I don't get it," whispered Captain Underpants. "The fuel tank now says SPRAY GUN, and the spray gun now says FUEL TANK, and the rapid-growth juice has been replaced with self-destruct juice... What's it all mean?"

"You'll find out," said Harold sadly.

When the three evil space guys had
finished laughing triumphantly, Jennifer
reached for the carton that read SUPER EVIL
RAPID-GROWTH JUICE and poured it into the
nozzle that read SPRAY GUN.

"Oh, I get it," said Captain Underpants.
"That space guy didn't pour growth juice
into the spray gun – he poured self-
destruct juice into the *fuel tank*!"

"Yep," George said sadly.

"And that means this spaceship thingy is
going to explode into millions of pieces!"

"Right," said Harold gloomily.

The spaceship began to sputter and shake as smoke billowed out of the control panels. Soon sparks were flying and ceiling tiles were falling.

Captain Underpants smiled proudly because he had figured out George's plan. But his smile didn't last long.

"Hey," he cried. "*WE'RE* in the space-ship thingy! What's gonna happen to *us*?"

"We had to sacrifice ourselves to save the world," said George. "I'm afraid we're not going to make it."

"*Of course* we'll make it," cried Captain Underpants. "We've got *Wedgie Power* on our side!"

CHAPTER 20

THE GREAT ESCAPE

Captain Underpants grabbed a roll of toilet paper from the jail cell lavatory.

"We can swing to safety on *this*!" he said.

"You can't *swing* on toilet paper," said Harold.

"Sure I can," said Captain Underpants. "I did it in my last comic book!"

Captain Underpants opened the jail cell window and tossed the toilet paper into a tall tree below them. "Come on, fellas," he said. "Let's swing out of here before this spaceship explodes!"

"That toilet paper won't hold you," said George. "It's not strong enough!"

"Sure it is," said Captain Underpants. "It's *two-ply*!"

George and Harold grabbed Captain
Underpants's cape. "Don't jump!" they cried.

But Captain Underpants wouldn't listen.
He jumped through the window with
George and Harold still clinging to his cape.

"AAAAAAAAAAAAAAAHGH!" they
screamed as they fell to the ground and
were killed instantly.

SPLAT

Just kidding.

Of course, the toilet paper could not support the weight of our three heroes, and for a moment, it looked like they were doomed.

But suddenly, Captain Underpants's red polyester cape opened up like a parachute – *PHOOOOP!*

George, Harold and the Waistband Warrior floated down safely as the spaceship above them exploded.

KA-BOOM!

"Hallelujah!" cried Harold. *"We're not gonna die!* WE'RE NOT GONNA DIE!"

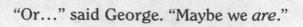

"Or…" said George. "Maybe we *are*."

CHAPTER 21

THE DELIRIOUSLY DANGEROUS DEATH-DEFYING DANDELION OF DOOM

George, Harold and Captain Underpants floated downwards, directly into the waiting jaws of the Dandelion of Doom.

"Aw, *man*!" cried Harold. "We *could* have got killed in a cool exploding spaceship. But instead, we're gonna get eaten by a *dandelion*. How *humiliating*!"

"Yeah," George moaned. "People are going to be giggling at our funerals."

The dandelion munched Captain Underpants and swung George and Harold around like a couple of rag dolls.

The two boys flew off and landed on the roof of the school.

"HELP MEEEeeEEEEeeEEEeeeEEE," screamed Captain Underpants as the Dandelion of Doom swung him back and forth.

"What should we do?" cried Harold.

"I've got an idea," said George. "It's a bad idea, and I know we're going to regret it, but we've got to act fast! The fate of the entire planet is in our hands."

The next time the giant evil dandelion
lurched towards the boys, George poured
some EXTRA-STRENGTH SUPER POWER JUICE
into Captain Underpants's mouth.

"What do you think is going to happen
now?" asked Harold.

"I don't know," said George. But I have a
feeling it's gonna involve incredibly graphic
violence!"

CHAPTER 22

THE INCREDIBLY GRAPHIC VIOLENCE CHAPTER, PART 2 (IN FLIP-O-RAMA™)

WARNING:

The following chapter contains scenes of a very unpleasant nature.

All nastiness was performed by a qualified stuntman and a licensed stuntplant. Do not attempt to battle giant evil dandelions at home, even if you have recently consumed EXTRA-STRENGTH SUPER POWER JUICE.

Such behavior could result in serious boo-boos.

– The National Board of Boo-Boo Prevention

FLIP-O-RAMA 4

(pages 383 and 385)

Remember, flip *only* page 383.
While you are flipping, be sure you
can see the picture on page 383
and the one on page 385.
If you flip quickly, the two
pictures will start to look like
<u>one</u> *animated* picture.

Don't forget to
add your own sound-effects!

LEFT HAND HERE

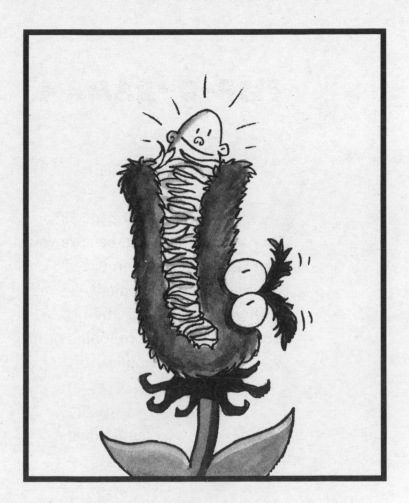

WHEN DANDELIONS ATTACK

RIGHT THUMB HERE

RIGHT
INDEX
FINGER
HERE

WHEN DANDELIONS ATTACK

FLIP-O-RAMA 5

(pages 387 and 389)

Remember, flip *only* page 387.
While you are flipping, be sure you
can see the picture on page 387
and the one on page 389.
If you flip quickly, the two
pictures will start to look like
<u>one</u> *animated* picture.

Don't forget to
add your own sound-effects!

LEFT HAND HERE

THE WEDGIE WEED
WHACKER

RIGHT
THUMB
HERE

RIGHT
INDEX
FINGER
HERE

THE WEDGIE WEED WHACKER

FLIP-O-RAMA 6

(pages 391 and 393)

Remember, flip *only* page 391.
While you are flipping, be sure you
can see the picture on page 391
and the one on page 393.
If you flip quickly, the two
pictures will start to look like
<u>one</u> *animated* picture.

Don't forget to
add your own sound-effects!

LEFT HAND HERE

HOORAY FOR CAPTAIN UNDERPANTS!

391

RIGHT
THUMB
HERE

HOORAY FOR CAPTAIN UNDERPANTS!

CHAPTER 23

THE TWENTY-THIRD CHAPTER

Captain Underpants (with the help of his newly developed super powers) had defeated the deliriously dangerous death-defying Dandelion of Doom! Now the only thing left to do was to stop the evil zombie nerds.

"Oh, *HOW* are we going to conquer the evil zombie nerds?" asked George. "How will we ever change them back to normal?"

"Well, we could try this ANTI-EVIL-ZOMBIE-NERD JUICE," said Harold.

George rolled his eyes. "I was hoping for something a *little* more dramatic," he said, "but we're running out of pages. Let's do it."

So Harold mixed up a batch of ANTI-EVIL-ZOMBIE-NERD ROOT BEER, and ordered everybody in the school to drink some.

The evil zombie nerds lined up. "Must drink root beer," they moaned. "Must drink root beer."

When the last zombie nerd had
swallowed his last sip of root beer, George
ordered Captain Underpants to get dressed
back up like Mr Krupp.

"But I'll lose my super powers if I put
on clothing," said Captain Underpants.
"The power of underwear must be—"

"Just put the clothes on!" George
instructed.

Captain Underpants did as he was told,
and then George poured water over the
hero's head.

"Now all we can do is wait," said Harold.
"Wait and hope that everybody returns to
normal."

CHAPTER 24

TO MAKE A LONG STORY SHORT

They did.

CHAPTER 25

BACK TO NORMAL?

"Hooray," said Harold. "It's great to have everybody back to normal."

"Yep," said George. "That's for sure."

But "back to normal" probably wasn't
the best choice of words. For while the
students and faculty were the same as
they'd always been, something had
definitely *changed* about Mr Krupp.

Because from that day on, whenever he heard the sounds of fingers snapping ...

SNAP!

Mr Krupp not only turned back into "you-know-who", but he also had *Extra-Strength Super Powers*.

And if you thought it was hard for
George and Harold to keep up with him
before, well…

... you ain't seen nothin' yet!

"OH, NO!" screamed Harold.

"HERE WE GO AGAIN!" screamed George.

ABOUT THE AUTHOR

When Dav Pilkey was a kid, his teachers
thought he was disruptive, "behaviourally
challenged", and in serious need of a
major attitude adjustment.

When he wasn't writing sentences in
the detention room, he could usually be
found sitting at his private desk out in the
hallway. There he spent his time writing and
drawing his own original comic books about
a superhero named Captain Underpants.

It was always Dav's dream to publish
a book about Captain Underpants.
Now that dream has come true . . .

Visit Dav Pilkey's Extra-Crunchy
Web Site O' Fun at:
www.pilkey.com

Novels With WEDGIE POWER!

CAPTAIN UNDERPANTS and the Perilous Plot of Professor Poopypants

Is it a bird? Is it a plane? NO — it's PANTS! George and Harold's Wedgie Wonder is back and now he's got Extra-Strength Super Powers!

And it looks like he's going to need them. Professor Pippy P. Poopypants, the dastardly new science teacher, is on the rampage for no reason at all (OK, George and Harold might have upset him just a little bit). He has the fiendish Shrinky-Pig 2000 and he's prepared to use it! Only Captain Underpants can stop Poopypants reducing the world to the size of a pair of pre-shrunk underpants!

CAPTAIN UNDERPANTS and the Wrath of the Wicked Wedgie Woman

George and Harold are having a normal kind of week. Yesterday they found out they were going to flunk fourth grade. Today they've created an evil, super-powerful monster. She's mean. She's got a fake-fur Evil Baddie costume (and she's having a really bad hair day). She's armed with ... yes, it's Spray Starch! The only weapon that can stop Captain Underpants in his fight for Truth, Justice and all that is Pre-Shrunk and Cottony!

The Adventures of SUPER DIAPER BABY

George Beard and Harold Hutchins are special. Yeah, ask their school principal, Mr Krupp (just make sure you aren't standing too close – he's got a mean right hook). Now the amazingly talented George and Harold have created an all-new superhero – Super Diaper Baby! The first newborn ever to fight crime, stomp on evil baddies and not get his diaper dirty. With the help of his trusty sidekick, Diaper Dog, little Billy Hoskins is out to save the world before bedtime!

Special guest appearance by CAPTAIN UNDERPANTS!

CAPTAIN UNDERPANTS and the Big, Bad Battle of the Bionic Booger Boy PART 1

George and Harold are in a sticky situation. Their latest prank has snotty school brainiac Melvin Sneedly seeing red, and he can't wait to get them back. But when Melvin tries to transform himself into a bionic-powered superboy, things get a little gloopy – and the Bionic Booger Boy is born! Can Captain Underpants beat this blobby behemoth of blech, or is the entire world doomed to drown in disgusting nose-dribble? Pass the tissues, please!

CAPTAIN UNDERPANTS and the Big, Bad Battle of the Bionic Booger Boy PART 2

Just when they thought they were safe, the terror starts all over again! Our heroes beat the Bionic Booger Boy, but they forgot about those rascally Robo-Boogers. Join George, Harold, Mr Krupp, Melvin Sneedly and Sulu the Bionic Hamster on an adventure that will take them into the deepest regions of outer space and back through time to the mysterious and uncharted world of the day before yesterday! It's a monster-mashin', robo-wranglin', time-travellin', brain-switchin', nose-pickin' good time!

The CAPTAIN UNDERPANTS Extra-Crunchy Book o' Fun

Join George and Harold and their wedgie-powered superhero, Captain Underpants, for more fun and games and hilarious pranks! Find out how to draw your favourite characters and how to make your very own comic books, complete with that world-famous cheesy animation technique, FLIP-O-RAMA! And fly by the seat of your pants as you pit your wits against Professor Poopypants and his Preposterous Puzzles of Perplexing Peril!

The All New CAPTAIN UNDERPANTS Extra-Crunchy Book o' Fun 2

They're back! The most disgusting jokes, the most perilous puzzles and the all-time silliest things to do EVER! George Beard and Harold Hutchins preeeeseeent ...

THE ALL NEW CAPTAIN UNDERPANTS EXTRA-CRUNCHY BOOK O' FUN 2! (Winner of longest and most ridiculous book title at the prestigious Strawberry Bottom Literary Festival.) Find out how to draw more of your favourite characters, and become the star of your own Captain Underpants adventure. And don't miss the brand new Hairy Potty comic — but be warned, it's packed full of violence, toilets and completely inappropriate humour...

FEATURING PUZZLES, ACTIVITIES AND ALL NEW COMICS!